Whose dark or troubled mind will you step into next? Detective or assassin, victim or accomplice? How can you tell reality from delusion when you're spinning in the whirl of a thriller, or trapped in the grip of an unsolvable mystery? When you can't trust your senses, or anyone you meet; that's when you know you're in the hands of the undisputed masters of crime fiction.

Writers of the greatest thrillers and mysteries on earth, who inspired those that followed. Their books are found on shelves all across their home countries – from Asia to Europe, and everywhere in between. Timeless tales that have been devoured, adored and handed down through the decades. Iconic books that have inspired films, and demand to be read and read again. And now we've introduced Pushkin Vertigo Originals – the greatest contemporary crime writing from across the globe, by some of today's best authors.

So step inside a dizzying world of criminal masterminds with **Pushkin Vertigo**. The only trouble you might have is leaving them behind.

FRIEDRICH DÜRRENMATT

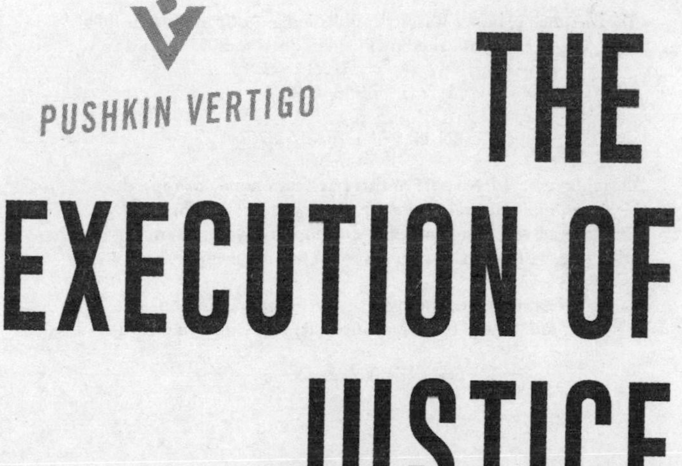

THE EXECUTION OF JUSTICE

TRANSLATED BY JOHN E. WOODS

Pushkin Press
71–75 Shelton Street
London, WC2H 9JQ

The Execution of Justice was first published as *Justiz* in Zurich, 1985
First published by Pushkin Press in 2017

1 3 5 7 9 8 6 4 2

ISBN 13: 978 1 782273 87 5

Text designed and typeset by Tetragon, London
Printed and bound by CPI Group (UK) Ltd, Croydon CRO 4YY

www.pushkinpress.com

THE EXECUTION OF JUSTICE

Granted, I'm putting all this down in an orderly report—it's the pedant in me maybe—so that the case can be closed. I want to force myself to go over one more time the events that led to the acquittal of a murderer and to the death of an innocent man. I want one more time to think through the steps I was lured into taking, the measures I took, the possibilities left undone. I want conscientiously to gauge whatever chances may still remain for the justice system. But above all I am writing this report because I have time, lots of time, two months at least. I've just returned from the airport (the bars I visited on the way don't count, nor is my present condition of any consequence. I am dead drunk, but I'll be sober in the morning). The huge machine, with Dr. *honoris causa* Isaak Kohler aboard, was rising into the night sky, howling, bellowing, toward Australia as I leapt from my VW, the safety off my revolver. It was one of his finest maneuvers to get that phone call through to me in time. Presumably the old man knew what I was up to; everybody knows I haven't got the money to follow him.

So I have no choice but to wait till he comes back, sometime, in June or July maybe, to wait, to get drunk now and then, or frequently, depending on my finances, and to write, the only appropriate activity for a lawyer whose career is a total shambles. But the canton deputy is mistaken about one thing: Time won't mend his crime, my waiting won't mitigate it, my being drunk won't blot it out, my writing won't excuse it. By presenting the truth, I'll fix it in my mind, enabling me at some point—in June, as I said, or in July or whenever he comes back (and he will come back)—to do deliberately, whether drunk or sober, what I was going to do just now purely on impulse. The report is meant not just to provide evidence of a murder but to prepare for one as well. For a just murder.

Sober and back again in my study: Justice can be restored only by a crime. That afterward I'll have to commit suicide is unavoidable. Not that I intend to avoid responsibility; on the contrary, it is the only responsible way to act—if not in a legal sense, then in a humane one. Possessing the truth, I cannot prove it. I lack witnesses to the critical moment. If I take my own life, it will make it easier for me to be believed even without witnesses. I do not approach death like some scientist executing himself in an experiment for the sake of science. I die because I have thought my situation through to its conclusion.

Scene of the Crime: It plays a role very early on. The Du Théâtre with its rococo façade is one of the few showpieces of our hopelessly overbuilt city. The restaurant is located on three floors, something not everyone knows, most people think there are only two. On the ground floor, as morning drags on—everybody is up early in this town—you find sleepy students, and business people as well, who then often stay through midday; later, after the coffee and kirsch, it gets quiet, the waitresses become invisible, and not until around four do the weary teachers drop by, the tired civil servants settle in. The crush, of course, arrives for dinner, and then, after ten-thirty, besides the politicians, managers, and creatures of finance, come the various representatives of the free professions, some very free, plus a few slightly shocked strangers—our city loves to put on international airs. On the second floor, then, everything turns so swanky it stinks. "Stink" is the right word for it: The two low rooms with their red wallpaper are like a steamy jungle, but people put up with it all the same, the women in evening gowns, the gentlemen often in black tie. The air is saturated with sweat, perfume, and more to the point, the odor of our city's culinary specialities, scallops of veal with home fries, etc. People meet here (essentially the same folks as downstairs, only in gala costume) after premieres and after big business deals, not to pull them off but to celebrate their having been pulled off. On the third floor, however, the character of the Du Théâtre changes all over again. You're taken aback by a whiff of dissipation. There's an ostentatious nonchalance. The rooms here are high and bright, look more like those of a cheap tavern—ordinary wooden chairs, checkered cloths on the tables, beer coasters everywhere, right beside the stairway a half-empty cabaret with mediocre magicians and even more mediocre strippers, people playing cards and billiards in the main room. Here sit our city's fruit-and-vegetable dealers, contractors and department store owners, auto sales execs and demolition experts, often for hours, making phenomenal bets, and the kibitzers crowd around them, odd and dubious characters, and there are always several hookers hanging around as well, three, four, of them, always at the same table by the window, more than just tolerated, they belong to the decor and come cheap. Relatively. Really rich people pay attention to the small change.

The first time I met the canton deputy, I had just taken my state exam, written my dissertation, been awarded my doctorate and admitted to the bar, but I was still working, as I had while a student, as a high-class gofer for Stüssi-Leupin. The latter had gained a reputation well beyond the borders of our country by the acquittals he had managed to get in the murder cases of the Ätti brothers, Rosa Pick, Deubelbeiss and Amsler, and by the agreement he had arranged between the Trög Amelioratory Works and the United States (very much to the advantage of the Trög party). I was to make a delivery to him at the Du Théâtre, a brief for one of those dubious cases that only he could love. I found the star lawyer on the third floor at the billiard table, where he had just ended a game with the canton deputy. Dr. Benno and Professor Winter were playing at another table, and only now as I write this does it occur to me that at that point the main characters of the drama to follow were assembled, as if in a prologue. It was very cold outside, November or December—I could easily determine the exact date—and I was frozen to the bone because as usual I wasn't wearing a coat and had had to park my Volkswagen several blocks away from the Du Théâtre.

"Have yourself a glass of grog, young man," the canton deputy said to me. He eyed me observantly and waved to a waiter. I obeyed automatically; besides, I had to wait for instructions from Stüssi-Leupin, who had gone off with the brief and was paging through it at his table. At the front of the room, the grocers were gambling, dark silhouettes against the front windows. The hollow trundling of the tram could be heard from the street. The canton deputy was still watching me, candidly, making no attempt to hide it. He might have been going on seventy. He was the only one who hadn't removed his jacket, wasn't even sweating. I finally introduced myself, suspecting that I was standing face-to-face with a man of some prominence, though I couldn't think of his name.

"Related to Colonel Spät?" he asked, without mentioning his own name, whether because he considered that unimportant or because he assumed I already knew it. (Colonel Spät: militaristic farmer, nowadays member of the federal cabinet. Demands atomic weapons.)

"Hardly," I answered. (To take care of this matter once and for all: I was born in 1930. I never knew my mother, Anna Spät; my father is unknown. I grew up in an orphanage and recall it fondly—especially the vast forest bordering it. The administration and the faculty were excellent, my youth happy; it is most decidedly not always an advantage to have parents. My misfortune began with Dr.h.c. Isaak Kohler. Before that I had some difficulties, true, but not hopeless ones.)

"You want to become Stüssi-Leupin's partner, do you?" he asked.

I looked at him in amazement. "Never entered my mind."

"He thinks a lot of you."

"Not so that I could notice thus far."

"Stüssi-Leupin never lets people notice," the old man observed dryly.

"His mistake," I answered casually. "I want to work for myself."

"That will be difficult."

"Possibly."

The old man laughed. "You are in for some surprises. It isn't easy to get to the top in this country. Do you play billiards?" he then asked out of the blue.

I replied I didn't.

"A mistake," he said, giving me the thoughtful eye all over again, gray eyes full of astonishment, but without mockery, or so it appeared, humorless and hard, and led me to the second table, where Dr. Benno and Professor Winter were playing. I knew them both, the professor from my university days—he was chancellor when I matriculated—Dr. Benno from our city's nightlife, which in those days went on only till midnight, but if for that reason alone, with some intensity. His profession was uncertain. He had once won an Olympic medal in fencing—which was why people called him Olympic Heinz—had once been Swiss master in pistol-shooting, and was still a well-known golfer; at one point he had run a gallery that hadn't turned a profit. Now it was said he mainly managed other people's fortunes.

I greeted them, they nodded.

"Winter will always be a greenhorn," said Dr.h.c. Kohler.

I laughed. "Meaning you're an expert?"

"But of course," he answered calmly. "Billiards is my passion. Give me the cue, Professor, you'll never make that shot."

Professor Adolf Winter gave him the billiard cue. He was in his sixties, a heavy man but of the shorter sort, with a gleaming bald head, gold rimless glasses, a well-kempt black beard with streaks of gray, which he kept stroking worthily, always impeccably dressed in a sophisticated conservative way, one of those liberal arts blowhards who populate our university, member of PEN and the Usteri Foundation, author of the two-volume tome *Carl Spitteler and Hesiod, or Switzerland and Greece: A Comparison* (Artemis, 1940). (The liberal arts faculty has always got on my lawyer's nerves.)

The canton deputy worked the leather tip carefully with the chalk. His movements were calm and sure, and however abrupt the shots he made, nothing about him seemed arrogant, simply deliberate and composed, all of it suggesting power and imperturbability. He regarded the billiard table with his head tilted slightly, then made his shot, decisive and quick.

I followed the rolling of the white balls, how they crashed against each other and bounced off.

"*A la bande.* That's how you have to beat Benno," the deputy said, as he handed the cue back to Professor Winter. "Got that, young man?"

"Don't know anything about it," I answered and turned to my grog, which the waiter had set down on a little table.

"You'll understand it someday all the same." Dr.h.c. Isaak Kohler laughed, taking a newspaper scroll from the wall rack and moving away.

The Murder: What happened three years later is public knowledge and will not take long to describe (nor do I have to be absolutely sober to do it). Dr.h.c. Isaak Kohler had already vacated his seat, although his party wanted to nominate him for canton senator (not for the federal cabinet, as several foreign newspapers had it), had withdrawn from politics entirely (and from his law practice long before that), was managing a brick trust that was more and more assuming worldwide dimensions, and was serving as president of various corporate boards, working as well for a UNESCO commission; sometimes you didn't see him around town for months. One unseemly springlike day in March of 1955, he was guiding B., a minister in the English cabinet, around the city. The minister had come on a private visit, had been treated in a private clinic for stomach tumors, and was now sitting beside the canton deputy emeritus in the latter's Rolls-Royce and reluctantly allowing himself to be shown the city, having firmly resisted for four weeks, only to yield now, was sitting there yawning at the sights as they slipped past, the Institute of Technology, the University, the Münster, "romanesque" (the deputy offered the catch phrases), the river quivered in the soft air (the sun was just setting), the quay was crowded with people. The minister nodded off, on his lips the taste of the countless servings of mashed potatoes and granola porridge that he had enjoyed in the private clinic, while dreaming of straight shots of whiskey, and hearing the voice of the deputy as if far in the distance, the rumble of traffic as an even more distant rustle; a leaden exhaustion lay within him and perhaps already the suspicion that the stomach tumors had not been benign after all.

"Just a moment," said Dr.h.c. Isaak Kohler and had Franz, his chauffeur, stop in front of the Du Théâtre, climbed out, instructed him to wait a minute, pointed mechanically with his umbrella at the "eighteenth-century" façade, but Minister B. did not react at all, dozed on, dreamed on. The deputy went into the restaurant, passing through the revolving door into the large dining room, where the maître d' greeted him respectfully. It was nearing seven, the tables were all occupied now, people eating dinner, voices babbling, lips licking, tableware clattering. The deputy emeritus looked about him, walked toward the middle of the dining room, where Professor Winter was sitting at a small table, busy with a tournedos rossini and a bottle of Chambertin, pulled out a revolver and shot the PEN Club member dead, not without having first greeted him amiably (the whole thing was played out in the most dignified fashion), then walked past the petrified maître d', who gaped at him speechlessly, and past the confused waitresses, who were scared to death, walked through the revolving door and out into the mild March evening, climbed into his Roll-Royce, sat down next to the dozing minister, who had noticed nothing, who hadn't even been aware that the car had stopped, who, as mentioned, was dozing on, dreaming on, whether of whiskey, or of politics (the Suez crisis later washed him away with it too), or of some definite premonition in regard to his stomach tumors (his death was announced last week in the papers, only briefly noted, and most of them were not all that scrupulous about the orthographics of his name).

"To the airport, Franz," Dr.h.c. Isaak Kohler ordered.

The Intermezzo of the Arrest: It cannot be related without a certain schadenfreude. Several tables away from the murdered man, the commandant of our canton police was dining with his old friend Mock, a deaf sculptor so self-absorbed that he took not the least notice of the whole incident, not even afterward. The two were sharing a pot-au-feu, Mock with satisfaction, the commandant, who did not like the Du Théâtre and visited it seldom, with an ill humor. Nothing tasted right: The broth was too cold, the stew meat too tough, the lingonberries too sweet. As the shot rang out, the commandant didn't look up—which is possible, at least so it's said—since he was just about to do some workmanlike sucking of bone marrow, but then he stood up after all, even tipping his chair over as he did, which, as a stickler for law and order, he set back upright. When he got to Winter, the latter was now lying in his tournedos rossini, his hand still clenched around the glass of Chambertin.

"Wasn't that Kohler just now?" the commandant asked the helpless maître d', who gaped at him, distraught and pale.

"Yes, sir. Indeed it was," he murmured.

The commandant regarded the murdered professor of Germanics with a thoughtful air, gazing gloomily down at the plate of fried potatoes and green beans, let his eyes glide across the bowl of tender lettuce, tomatoes, and radishes.

"Well, there's nothing more to be done," he said.

"Yes, sir. Indeed not."

The guests, at first spellbound, had sprung to their feet. The cook and the kitchen crew stared over from behind the counter. Only Mock went on eating calmly. A lanky man pushed his way forward.

"I'm a doctor."

"Don't touch him," the commandant ordered calmly. "We have to photograph him first."

The doctor bent down to the professor but obeyed the order.

"Yes, indeed," he determined. "Dead."

"Precisely," the commandant answered calmly. "Go back to your table."

Then he removed the bottle of Chambertin from the table.

"That's requisitioned," he said and handed it to the maître d'.

"Yes, sir. Indeed it is," he muttered.

And then the commandant went to do some telephoning.

When he returned, Public Prosecutor Jämmerlin was already beside the corpse. He was wearing a formal dark suit. He had been on his way to attend a symphony concert at the Tonhalle and had just consumed an omelette flambée in the French restaurant on the second floor when he heard the shot. Jämmerlin was not well liked. Everyone yearned for him to retire, both the prostitutes and their competition from the other camp, the thieves and burglars, treacherous junior partners, businessmen in difficulty; and the legal authorities—from the police on through the lawyers, even his own colleagues—had deserted him as well. Everyone told jokes about him: It was no wonder things were jammed up in this town; since Jämmerlin was in office, the justice system couldn't get jammed up any worse, etc. The prosecutor was playing a losing game, his authority had long since been undermined, and his particular cross was the commandant, who, so people said, regarded the so-called criminal element of our population as its more valuable segment. And yet, Jämmerlin was a lawyer in the grand style—he didn't always come out on the short end, his indictments and objections were feared, his uncompromising nature was so impressive that people hated him. He was the very picture of an attorney of the old school, personally offended by every acquittal, equally unfair to rich and poor, a bachelor, untroubled by any temptation, never once having touched a woman. Most detrimental, professionally speaking. Criminals were something beyond his comprehension, something downright satanic, who set him into an Old Testament rage; he was a relic of an unyielding but equally incorruptible morality, an erratic block in the "morass of a justice system that pardons all offenses," as he expressed it with a vigor that matched his rage. And he was also extraordinarily agitated at the moment, all the more so since he was personally acquainted with both the murdered man and the murderer.

"Commandant," he shouted with outrage, his napkin still in his hand, "they tell me Dr. Isaak Kohler committed this murder!"

"Correct," the commandant answered testily.

"That's simply impossible!"

"Kohler must have gone crazy," the commandant answered, taking a seat on a chair beside the dead man and lighting one of his everlasting Bahianos. The prosecutor dried his brow with his napkin, pulled a chair over from the next table, likewise took a seat, so that the huge corpse now lay, head on plate, between the two massive, heavy officials. And so they waited. Deathly silence in the restaurant. No one was eating now. Everyone stared at the ghostly group. But then a fraternity entered the room, and confusion reigned. Singing loudly, they took over the place and, since they did not realize the situation right off, went on singing at full strength, then fell silent in embarrassment. Finally Lieutenant Herren arrived with his staff from the homicide squad. A policeman took pictures, a forensic physician stood around helplessly, and a local prosecuting attorney who had been brought along kept apologizing to Jämmerlin for being there. Orders, instructions in low tones. Then the dead man was set upright, gravy in his face, foie gras and green beans in his beard, laid on a stretcher, and put in the ambulance. It was Ella who, once she was allowed to clear the table, first discovered his gold rimless glasses in the home fries. And then the first witnesses were questioned by the local prosecuting attorney.

Possible Conversation I: As the waitresses came back to life and the guests slowly and hesitantly sat back down, some of them beginning to eat again, as the first journalists started to move in, the public prosecutor and the commandant withdrew to the pantry next to the kitchen for a conference. The prosecutor wanted to speak with the commandant alone for a moment, with no witnesses. A Last Judgment had to be organized and carried out. The brief conversation next to shelves of bread, canned food, bottled oil, and sacked flour took an unfortunate course. According to the account that the commandant later gave before parliament, the prosecutor demanded a massive deployment of police.

"What for?" the commandment objected. "Anyone acting the way Kohler did is not about to flee. We can quietly arrest him at home."

Jämmerlin became more emphatic. "I can expect, I presume, that you will treat Kohler like any other criminal."

The commandant was silent.

"The man is one of the richest and best-known citizens of this city," Jämmerlin continued. "It is our sacred duty" (one of his favorite turns of phrase) "to proceed with the utmost rigor. We must avoid every appearance of partiality."

"It is our sacred duty to avoid unnecessary expenses," the commandant declared calmly.

"No all-points bulletin?"

"I wouldn't think of it."

The prosecutor stared at the bread-slicer he was standing

next to. "You're a friend of Kohler's," he suggested finally, not maliciously at all, simply routinely and coldly. "Do you not think it possible that under the circumstances your objectivity might suffer?"

Silence. "Lieutenant Herren," the unruffled commandant answered, "will take over the Kohler case."

And that's how the scandal came about.

Herren was a man of action, ambitious and thus overhasty when he acted. He succeeded within a few minutes in alarming not only the entire police force but the whole population as well, managing to launch a special report of the canton police just before the seven-thirty radio news. The apparatus was moving full steam ahead. They found Kohler's villa empty (he was a widower, his daughter, a stewardess with Swissair, was in the clouds, his cook at the movies). They concluded he was attempting to flee. Patrol cars stalked the streets, border stations were informed, foreign police forces notified. From a purely technical standpoint, all this was quite praiseworthy, except that they were forgetting the one contingency that the commandant had suspected all along: They were searching for a man who had no intention of fleeing. And so disaster had already struck when, shortly after eight, news came in from the airport that Kohler had delivered the English minister to his plane and then had been driven at a leisurely pace back to the city in his Rolls-Royce. The prosecutor was hit especially hard. Reassured that the mighty machinery of state was functioning, and buoyant following his victory over the detested commandant, he was getting ready to listen to the overture to Mozart's *Abduction from the Seraglio,* was stroking his cropped gray beard with great pleasure as he leaned back in his seat. Mondschein had just raised his baton when, at the side of one of the richest and also most unsuspecting widows of our fair city, the Dr.h.c., sought and hunted with every modern device known to the police, came striding down the center aisle of the Tonhalle, past the packed rows of the audience, calm and self-assured as ever, with the most innocent air, as if nothing had happened, and sat down beside Jämmerlin, even shaking the incredulous man's hand. The stir, the whispers and, sad to say, the giggles as well were considerable, the overture fell not unnoticeably flat, since the orchestra had taken note of the event; one curious oboist even stood up, Mondschein had to give the downbeat twice, and the prosecutor was so flummoxed that he sat there frozen stiff, not just for the *Seraglio* overture but for the second piano concerto of Johannes Brahms, which followed. He did, it is true, finally comprehend the nature of the situation, but only after the pianist had started in; then, not daring to interrupt the Brahms, his respect for culture being too great, he was painfully aware that he ought to have intervened, and that now it was too late, and so he sat there until intermission. Then he acted. He shoved his way through the curious crowd encircling the canton deputy and ran to the telephone booth but had to come back to get some change from one of the women checking coats. He called the police station, got hold of Herren, a major deployment came swooping down. Meanwhile Kohler played the unsuspecting innocent, buying the widow champagne at the bar, and even had the outrageous good luck of the concert's second half beginning before the police arrived. So that Jämmerlin, along with Herren, had to wait behind closed doors, while inside Bruckner's Seventh was presented, endlessly. The prosecutor stomped back and forth irritably, had to be reminded several times by an usherette to keep quiet, and was generally treated as if he were a barbarian. He cursed the entire Romantic movement, cursed Bruckner, they still hadn't got beyond the adagio, and when finally at the end of the fourth movement the applause began—it likewise seeming to know no end—and the audience came streaming out through the cordon of deployed police, no Dr.h.c. Isaak Kohler appeared. He had vanished. The commandant had ushered him through the artists' exit and into his car and had driven with him to police headquarters.

Possible Conversation II: At police headquarters, the commandant took the Dr.h.c. to his office. They had not spoken a word to each other during the drive, and the commandant led the way down the empty, dimly lit corridor. In his office he pointed without speaking to a comfortable leather armchair, bolted the door, took off his jacket.

"Make yourself comfortable," he said.

"Thanks, I'm already comfortable," the canton deputy answered, having taken a seat.

The commandant placed two glasses on the table between the two armchairs, fetched a bottle of red wine from the cupboard. "Winter's Chambertin," he declared and poured, sat down himself, stared into space for a while, then began carefully to wipe the sweat from his brow and the back of his neck.

"Dear Isaak," he finally began, "tell me for heaven's sake why you shot that old ass."

"You mean—" the canton deputy answered somewhat hesitantly.

"Have you any clear notion of what you've done?" the commandant interrupted him.

The other man took a long, slow drink from his glass and did not answer on the spot, instead regarding the commandant with some astonishment, but with gentle mockery as well.

"But of course," he then said. "But of course I've a clear notion."

"All right, why did you shoot Winter?"

"Ah, I see," the canton deputy answered and appeared to ponder something, then laughed. "Ah, so that's it. Not bad."

"What's not bad?"

"The whole thing."

The commandant didn't know what to reply, was confused, angry. Whereas the murderer had turned downright cheerful, laughing to himself softly several times, apparently amused for some incomprehensible reason.

"Well. Why did you murder the professor?" the commandant began questioning him stubbornly again, insistently, and again wiping sweat from his neck and brow.

"I have no reason," the canton deputy admitted.

The commandant stared at him, perplexed, thinking he hadn't heard right, then emptied his glass of Chambertin, poured himself some more, spilling some wine.

"No reason?"

"None."

"That's utter nonsense, you must have some reason," the commandant shouted impatiently. "That's utter nonsense!"

"I beg you, do you duty," Kohler said and carefully emptied his glass.

"My duty is to arrest you," the commandant explained.

"Just so."

The commandant was desperate. He loved clarity in all things. He was a sensible fellow. To him, a murder was an accident over which he pronounced no moral judgment. But as an orderly man he had to have a reason. A murder without a motive was for him not a contravention of morals but definitely one of logic. And there was no such thing.

"The best thing would be for me to put you in an asylum for observation," he declared in a rage. "There is no such thing as your committing murder for no reason."

"I'm quite normal," Kohler responded coolly.

"Shall I call Stüssi-Leupin?" the commandant suggested.

"What for?"

"You need a defense lawyer, for chrissake. The best we have, and Stüssi-Leupin is the best."

"A public defender will do for me."

The commandant gave up. He unbuttoned his collar, took a deep breath.

"You must be crazy," he gasped. "Give me the revolver."

"What revolver?"

"The one you shot the professor with."

"Don't have it," the Dr.h.c. declared and stood up.

"Isaak," the commandant implored, "I hope you'll spare us a body search!"

He was about to pour himself some more wine. The bottle was empty.

"That damned Winter drank too much," the commandant growled.

"So get on with it, have them march me off," the murderer proposed.

"As you like," the commandant responded, "and you'll be spared no indignity." He got up as well, unbolted the door, then rang.

"Take this man away," he said to the policeman as he entered. "He's under arrest."

Belated Suspicion: In trying to reproduce these conversations—"possible" because I was not personally present for them—I do so not with the intention of writing a novel but rather from the necessity of delineating an event as faithfully as possible. But that is not the real difficulty. The wheels of justice turn, in fact, behind the scenes for the most part, and behind the scenes jurisdictional authorities that seem so clearly defined to the outside world become blurred, roles are exchanged or divided up differently, conversations occur between people who appear in public as irreconcilable enemies—on the whole, a different tone is predominant. Not everything gets put down in black and white and added to the records. Information is handed on or suppressed. And so, for instance, the commandant has always been candid with me, talkative, telling me everything voluntarily, letting me have a look at important documents, and often going beyond his authority, and even today is generally well-disposed toward me. Why, even Stüssi-Leupin was quite civil to me, even long after I had joined the other camp; only recently the wind has shifted, though for a totally different reason, to be sure. So that I don't have to invent these conversations, but rather to reconstruct them. At worst, to surmise them.

No, my "auctorial" difficulties lie elsewhere. Though I am well aware that even the murder and suicide I'm planning can provide no strict proof of my credibility, nevertheless, I continue to be seized by the mad hope that I can establish it by recording these events: by discovering, for instance, how Kohler's revolver was disposed of. The murder weapon has never been found. At first, a secondary matter. It played no role at the trial. There was no doubt who the culprit was, there had been witnesses enough: the staff and customers of the Du Théâtre. And though at the start of the investigation the commandant left no stone unturned to recover the revolver, he did so not to further incriminate Kohler—for which there was no need whatever—but for the sake of order; it was part of his criminological style, so to speak. But the commandant had no success. Inexplicably. Dr.h.c. Kohler's route from the Du Théâtre to the Tonhalle was known, its tiniest details verified. As we know, after shooting the professor in mid-gulp of tournedos rossini, he had immediately climbed into his Rolls-Royce and sat down beside the minister, floating mid-dream in whiskey. At the airport, the murderer and the minister got out of the car, the chauffeur (who of course knew nothing of the crime) did not notice a revolver, nor did the Swissair official who had hurried over to greet them. They had chatted in the lobby, dutifully admiring the architecture, or better, its interior design, then sauntered to the plane, with Kohler giving the minister a helping hand. Formal farewell, return with the official to the lobby, a final brief glance at the taxiing plane, a purchase at the kiosk, *Neue Zürcher Zeitung* and *National-Zeitung,* traversal of the lobby, still in the company of the Swissair man, though without a glance at the interior design, then into the waiting car, from the airport to Zollikerstrasse, two honks of the horn in front of the house of the unsuspecting widow, who appeared at once (time pressed), from Zollikerstrasse straight to the Tonhalle. No trace of the weapon. The widow had not noticed anything either. The revolver had vanished in thin air. The commandant ordered a meticulous search of the Rolls-Royce, then of the route Kohler had followed, plus his villa, his garden, the cook's room, the chauffeur's apartment on Freiestrasse. Nothing. The commandant pressed Kohler several times, thundered, tried hour-long interrogation. In vain. The Dr.h.c. passed with flying colors; only Hornusser, the pretrial judge who took over the interrogation, suffered a collapse. Then a protest from the prosecutor that the police and the pretrial judge needn't be so pedantic—with revolver, without revolver, it was not all that important, to continue the search was a waste of taxpayers' money, the commandant and the pretrial judge would have to abandon the search; and the vanished weapon took on meaning only later, via Stüssi-Leupin. That the weapon instills me with new hope these days is another story, is part of the difficulty of my enterprise. My role as Savior of Justice is a wretched one. I can do nothing but write, and if in the distance I spot some other possible way to intervene, some other mode of action, I abandon my Hermes portable, run to my car (a VW again now), start it up, roar off—like the day before yesterday, in the morning, to see the personnel manager of Swissair. An idea had struck me, a grand solution. I drove in a frenzy, it was a miracle that I reached the airport unhurt, and that others were unhurt. But the personnel manager would give me no information, wouldn't even see me. The return trip proceeded at a moderate tempo; at one intersection a policeman yelled at me: Did I intend to push my car through town? I felt as if once again I had played out my hand. It was impossible to hire Lienhard, the private detective, for further research; he cost too much and would, well, as things stood, probably not be interested—who gladly slices into his own flesh? So there was nothing for it but to try Hélène herself. I called her. Was out. Had "gone into town." So I just take off, hit or miss, on foot, think, check the restaurants or the bookstores, and I run into her, right into her, except she's sitting with Stüssi-Leupin, in front of the Select, having a cappuccino. I saw the two of them only at the last moment, was standing right in front of them, in some confusion, since I had been looking for her only, and angry that Stüssi-Leupin was sitting with her, but what difference did it make, the two had probably been lying in the same bed together for a good while, the sweet daughter of a murderer and her father's savior, she my former lover, he my former boss.

"If you please, Fräulein Kohler," I said, "I'd like to have a word with you for a moment. Alone."

Stüssi-Leupin offered her a cigarette, put one in his own mouth too, lit them.

"Is that all right with you, Hélène?" he asked her. I could have punched the star lawyer.

"No," she answered without looking at me, although she did put down the cigarette. "But he can speak if he likes."

"Good," I said, pulling over a chair and ordering an espresso.

"What do you want now, worthy genius of the law?" Stüssi-Leupin asked amiably.

"Fräulein Kohler," I said, barely able to hide my agitation, "I have a question for you."

"Please." She went on smoking.

"Ask it," Stüssi-Leupin suggested.

"At the time your father took the English minister to his plane, were you still a stewardess?"

"Certainly."

"And on board the plane that flew the minister back to England?"

She put out her cigarette.

"Possibly," she said.

"Thank you, Fräulein Kohler," I said and got up, offered my regards, left my espresso undrunk, and departed. I now knew how the weapon could have disappeared. It was all so simple. How silly. The old man had stuck it in the minister's coat pocket as he sat next to him in the Rolls-Royce, and his daughter, Hélène, had plucked the revolver from the coat pocket on the plane. That would have been easy for her as a stewardess. But now that I knew it, I felt empty and weary, drifted along down the quay, endlessly, with the stupid lake and its swans and sailboats on my right. If my theory was correct—and it had to be—Hélène was an accomplice. As guilty as her father. Meaning she had left me in the lurch, had had to know that I was right. Meaning her father had already won. He had proved stronger than I. Arguing with Hélène was pointless, because she had already decided, because the outcome was already decided. I could not force her to betray her father. What appeal could I make to her? To her ideals? What ideals? To the truth? She had suppressed it. To love? She had betrayed me. To justice? To which she would reply: Justice for whom? For a local giant of the intellect? Ashes rest easy. For a weak-kneed, lying skirt-chaser? He's been cremated, too. For me? Not worth the trouble. Justice is not a private matter. And then she would ask me: And why justice? For society in general? Just one more scandal, just stuff for gossip—come the day after tomorrow and other things will be the order of the day. Result of my cogitation: The value of justice did not weigh as heavily for Hélène as did her father. An enervating revelation for a lawyer. Should I therefore drag God into the affair? An admirable gentleman, no doubt, but pretty much a stranger of dubious existence. And then: What all the fellow had to worry about! (Measurement of the universe à la de Sitter—obsolete, much too modestly calculated—in centimeters: a one with twenty-eight zeros.) But the crux was to carry on, pull myself together, choke the philosophy back down, go right on with my battle against society, against Kohler, against Stüssi-Leupin—and take up battle with Hélène. Thinking is a nihilistic trait, putting all values in question, and so I doughtily turned back to the active life, wandered back into the center of town refreshed—lake, swans and sailboats on my left now—past lovers and pensioners, illumined most curiously and pleasantly by a sunset—drank Klävner right on through the evening (a wine I don't handle well at all), and when, around one o'clock, I disappeared with a rather notorious but nonetheless saliently built lady into her apartment house, there at the entrance stood Stuber from the vice squad, jotting down addresses, bowing courteously—the gesture was meant ironically, I suppose, hot coals on the head of a dissipated lawyer. A piece of bad luck. Possibly. (But the lady herself was decent enough, it was an honor, she said, I could pay next time, about which I expressed my doubts, confessing that next time as well I would hardly be in a position to pay, and admitting my profession, whereupon she hired me.)

My Country and Its People: A few remarks are unavoidable. A murder brings its ambience with it, its nearer and farther environs, the yearly average temperature, the mean frequency of earthquakes, and the human climate. All of this is interwoven. The enterprise that sometimes goes by the name of our country, sometimes by that of fatherland, was founded a little more than twenty generations ago, roughly calculated. Region: At first it was, for the most part, a play of limestone, granite, and molasse, with the addition of later Tertiary phenomena. Climate: Tolerable. History: At first mediocre, the Hapsburgian dynasty set itself abrewing, law-of-the-jungle chiefly, the idea was to club your way to the top, and club they did, cracked open knights, cloisters, and castles as if they were safes, prodigious plundering, booty, no prisoners taken, prayers before battle and orgies after slaughter, huge drinking bouts, war was profitable; but then, unfortunately, came the invention of gunpowder, big-power politics met with evergrowing resistance, thrashings with halberds and spiked clubs found their limits, close-quarter soldiers were banged silly from a distance; after less than eight generations, then, the famous retreat, followed by another seven generations of relative savagery, in part a matter of people murdering one another, subjugating peasants (freedom was never taken too seriously) and battling over religion, in part a matter of hiring out as mercenaries on the grand scale, spending blood for the highest bidder, protecting petty princes from the citizenry and all of Europe from freedom.

Then finally the storm of the French Revolution gathered, the hated Guards were mowed down as they bravely fought a forlorn fight in the service of a system gone rotten by the grace of God, while one of their aristocratic officers sat secure in his garret and penned poetry: "Forests now are dappled, stubblefields turned gold, and autumn has begun." A little later, Napoleon made a final clean sweep of all that rubbish about gracious lords and vassal states. Defeat was good for the nation. The rudiments of democracy appeared and new ideas: Pestalozzi, poor, shabby, and hot with passion, moved about the country, from one misfortune to another. A radical shift to commerce and trade began, draped in the appropriate ideals. Industries began to show their stuff, railroads were built. To be sure, the earth was not rich in natural treasures, coal and ore had to be imported and processed, but everywhere there was antlike diligence, growing wealth, but without any waste, nor, sad to say, any brilliance. Thrift established itself as the greatest virtue; banks were founded, at first hesitantly; debts were considered a disgrace; where once mercenaries had been the chief article of export, now came the bankrupts: Whoever went on the rocks had another chance across the ocean. Everything had to turn a profit and turn one it did, even the boundless heaps of stone and gravel-slides, the glacier tips and precipices. For once nature had been discovered and every idiot could feel sublime in mountain solitude, the tourist industry became possible. Our country's ideals were always practical ones. And for the rest, the populace lived so encapsulated that every conceivable foe found it more useful to leave them in peace—an immoral but healthy mode of life, granted, revealing little grandeur but considerable political common sense. People molted their way through two world wars, maneuvered between the beasts, always got out with their hide. Our generation appeared.

The Present (A.D. 1957): Major segments of the population live their lives away with hardly a care, secure and insured; churches, education, and hospitals are available at moderate cost, cremation ensues, if need be, without charge. Life glides along on solid tracks, but the past rattles the edifice, shakes the foundations. He who has much fears he will lose much. People climb down from their horses after some danger has passed like the proverbial rider after his ride over ice-covered Lake Constance. People are too timid to see that their own intelligence is a necessity, they can no longer accept the fact that they have been, if not heroes, at least reasonable; they rank themselves among the victors, the saga of warlike ancestors rises up, and out of those myths comes the danger of a short circuit; people dream of the ancient battles, rewrite the epics with themselves as fighters in the resistance, and behold! here comes the general staff conjuring up a world of Nibelungen, dreaming of atomic weapons, of a heroic war of extermination in event of attack, the goal of the army is to prepare the way for the end of the nation, root and branch, inexorable and final, while all around peoples subjugated long ago learn ways to squeak through with courage and cunning. But wait, the probable end may be taking another, droller course. Foreigners are buying up the land that people are out to defend, the economy's momentum is in alien hands and only administered by native ones; paying hardly any taxes, the citizenry is forming itself into an upper class, while below them thrifty and diligent Italians, Greeks, Spaniards, Portuguese, and Turks—often penned up together in quarters for which they pay shameless rent—are taking root, despised to some extent, often still illiterate, helots (indeed, in the eyes of their masters, subhumans) who, once they have become an aware proletariat, confident of its own vitality, may loftily demand their rights, in certain knowledge that half of the shares of the corporation that calls itself our nation have already been bought up by foreign capital and that it is dependent solely on them. In reality our little country, so people suspect, rubbing their amazed eyes, withdrew from history when it went into big business.

The Reaction of the Public: Against this background, the murder committed by the Dr.h.c. stood out in relief. Its effect could be calculated: Since we have depoliticized our politics—in this regard we point to the future, only in this are we truly modern, true pioneers, the world will either perish or be Swissified—since, then, nothing can be expected from our politicians, no miracles, no new life, only some gradually improved highways, since the country is behaving in a biologically refreshing fashion and refraining from conceiving children (that we are not numerous is a great asset, that our race is slowly improving thanks to our foreign workers, our greatest), every interruption in the daily rat race is greeted with gratitude, any diversion is welcomed, particularly since the stiff, dignified annual procession of our guilds can in no way provide a substitute for the carnival we lack. Dr.h.c. Isaak Kohler's deed had, then, a liberating effect, people could laugh unofficially at something at which they were officially outraged, and already on the evening of Professor Winter's demise, the rumor spread—ascribed to a high official in city government if not to the city president himself—that Kohler deserved another honorary doctorate for having prevented Winter's next speech on the First of August. Likewise, the bungled actions of the police yielded hardly any added moral outrage, the schadenfreude was simply too great. The relation between the populace and the police is strained; for some time now our city has not lived up to its reputation in that regard. Having unexpectedly become a metropolis, it wants to preserve the coziness, the middle-class sedulity, the virtue it always ascribed to itself, continues to ascribe, wants to remain personally impersonal, in the grip of tradition, even though tradition has long since gone to hell. Time has grown mightier than the city, for all her diligent deportment, it does with her what it will. And so we are neither the people we once were nor those we now need to be, we live at war with the present, do not want to do what we must do, obstinately never quite doing what must be done, but at best only doing things halfway, and even that grudgingly. The outward expression of our miseries is the growth of police operations, for he who lives at war with the present regiments things. Our community has for the most part become a police state that interferes in everything, in our morals and in our traffic (both in a chaotic state). The police are a symbol not so much of protection as of bullying. Enough. Under heavy influence of alcohol. Besides, the lady from the apartment has just entered my office (I'm back in my garret on Spiegelgasse), needs the protection of the law. I'll advise her to get a dog. She can take it and herself out for two walks per night (recommendation of the humane society, accepted by Jämmerlin with much gnashing of the teeth).

Prosecutor Jämmerlin: He hated the canton deputy. The fellow's nonchalance grated on his nerves. He could never forgive Kohler for having shaken his hand in the Tonhalle. He hated him so much that he found himself at variance with himself. The tension between his hate and his sense of justice had become unbearable. He considered declaring himself biased, but then again, he hoped the canton deputy would object to his serving as prosecutor. In his perplexity he confided in Chief Justice Jegerlehner. The chief justice sounded out the pretrial judge, who sounded out the commandant, who sighed and had the deputy brought to his office from the district jail, just to make things more sociable. The Dr.h.c. was in the best of moods. The Cheval-blanc was splendid. The commandant approached him again about Stüssi-Leupin, adding that his public defender was a notorious washout. Kohler replied that that was of no consequence. The commandant finally came around to the issue of Jämmerlin's scruples. The canton deputy assured him that he could not imagine a more impartial prosecutor, an answer which, when passed on to Jämmerlin, elicited a cry of rage, he'd show the canton deputy now, would bury him for life, whereupon the chief justice came close to dismissing the prosecutor but let matters rest for fear that in his fury the latter would have a stroke—Jämmerlin, he knew, was not in the best of health.

The Trial: It took place before five appellate judges of the appellate court, an early trial by our standards, in nothing flat, so to speak, one year after the murder, again in March. The crime had been committed in public; who the murderer was need not be proved. There was, however, no way to settle on a motive. There appeared to have been none. They could get nothing out of the canton deputy. They stood before an enigma. Even the painstaking interrogation of the accused by the judge whose task that was failed to bring the least indication to light. Relations between murderer and murdered could not have been more correct. They were involved in no business relationship, jealousy was out of the question, there weren't even conjectures in that regard. In view of this strange fact, there were two interpretations: Dr.h.c. Isaak Kohler was either mentally ill or an amoral monster who murdered for the pure joy of killing. The public defender, Lüthi, took the former position, Prosecutor Jämmerlin the latter; contradicting the former was the patent fact that Kohler made a thoroughly normal impression, contradicting the latter, his glorious past—a politician and captain of industry was of necessity a man of lofty morals. Besides which, for years he had been praised for his leanings toward policies of social (not socialistic) improvement. But this was Jämmerlin's most ambitious case. The hate, the ignominy, the jokes told at his expense, gave the old lawyer wings, the judges were no match for his irresistible momentum, the colorless Lüthi proved ineffective. To everyone's astonishment, Jämmerlin's theory of Kohler as inhuman monster prevailed. The five judges believed they had to set an example, even Jegerlehner yielded. Once again everything was done to preserve the façade of morality. The people, so the argument of the verdict read, must not only expect and demand morally impeccable conduct from the financially and socially privileged classes, but also be able to see that conduct lived out. The canton deputy was sentenced to twenty years in prison. Not quite a life sentence, just practically a life sentence.

Kohler's Behavior: Everyone was impressed with the accused murderer's dignity. He entered the courtroom well rested, having spent his pretrial detention primarily at a psychiatric clinic on Lake Constance, governed by some loose police regulation to be sure, but under the care of Professor Habersack, a close personal friend. He was allowed to move about; the caddy on the golf course was the village constable. When finally brought before the appellate court, Kohler rejected all preferential treatment, demanding "to be handled like an ordinary man of the people." The start of the trial was itself typical. The Dr.h.c. fell ill, the flu, the thermometer climbed to 102 degrees, he rejected any postponement, refused to use an invalid's chair in the courtroom. To the five judges he declared (trial transcript): "Here I stand, so that you can pass judgment on me according to your consciences and the law. You know what I have been accused of. Fine. Now it is for you to judge and for me to submit to your verdict. I will acknowledge it as just, however it may turn out." After the verdict, he was deeply moved and thanked them for the humane manner in which he had been treated, even thanked Jämmerlin. Actually, people listened to these effusions with more amusement than compassion; the general impression was that in Dr. Isaak Kohler's case the rolling wheels of justice had set an exceptional example, and as he was led away, the curtain seemed to have fallen on an unambiguous, though not thoroughly elucidated, affair.

Concerning Myself, Then and Now: This, then, the rough outline of the background, disappointing, I know, an event that came with the day, remarkable only for its participants and for those more intimately informed about it, the basis for gossip, for more-or-less tired jokes and for a few moralistic reflections on the crisis of Western civilization and democracy, a criminal case, dutifully reported by court reporters and commented upon by the editor in chief of our world-famous local paper (a friend of Kohler's) with customary national dignity, the topic of conversation for a few days, hardly the stuff to go much beyond the city limits, a provincial scandal that quite rightly would soon have been forgotten had there not been a plot hidden behind it. That I was to play a decisive role in that plot is my own bit of bad luck, though I must also admit I smelled something rotten from the start. But at this point I have to insert a few words about the state of my own affairs after Kohler's trial. Their state was not all that happy even then. I had tried to set myself up on my own after all and had established an office on Spiegelgasse, above the assembly hall of the Saints of Uetli, a pietist sect, in a room whose roof slanted toward its three windows, with a few armchairs grouped in front of a desk from Pfister Furnishings, with "aerial view" prints on the walls—I prefer to pass over the wallpaper—and with a telephone that was not yet functioning: a hole-in-the-wall that had been created when the owner had torn out the wall between two garrets and had had one of the two doors bricked up. The third garret was inhabited by Simon Berger, the preacher and founder of the Uetli sect, who looked like Saint Nicholas of Flüe and with whom I shared the corridor toilet. Granted, my office was situated ever so romantically, Büchner and Lenin had lived in the neighborhood, and the view out to the chimneys and television antennas of the old city stirred your admiration for the hometown, making you feel cozy in your own little parlor, lusting to start a cactus window-garden—and yet it was as unsuitable as imaginable for a lawyer, not just because it is difficult to reach by car, but because the cubbyhole is well-nigh impossible to ferret out: no elevator, steep creaky stairs, a rat's nest of corridors. (Addendum: At the time, this office site was inconvenient, but I was ambitious then, wanted to get a foot in the door, get ahead, become a respectable citizen; nowadays, for the down-at-the-heel specialist in whores that I have in fact become, this closet has proved ideal, even though the built-in couch makes it frightfully cramped; I sleep, screw, live, even cook here now, surrounded by the nocturnal drone of the psalms of the Saints of Uetli, "Search thy heart, O Christian man, save thy soul immortal, save, oh, save whate'er thou can, become a sinless mortal." At any rate, Lucky, the fellow who protects the lady of remarkable build and aboriginal profession and who just now dropped by, partly to satisfy his curiosity and partly to take care of some business problems and study the general situation, was of the jovial opinion that you could really breathe in here.) And so, even back then, clients stayed away in droves, I was essentially unemployed, had nothing to work on except a few shoplifting cases, debt collections, and the bylaws of the Prisoners' Gymnastic Club (a commission from the Department of Justice), soon took to lazing about, sometimes on the green banks of the quay, sometimes in front of the Café Select, played chess (with Lesser, both of us insisting on the Spanish opening, so that for the most part it was always the same game ending in stalemate), dined on an unimaginative but not unhealthy diet in the restaurants of our ladies' clubs. Under such circumstances, I could hardly afford to reject Kohler's letter requesting me to visit him in prison at R.; not that the request didn't seem somewhat fishy, since I couldn't imagine what the old man could want with an unknown, unestablished attorney, and also because I was afraid of being dominated by him; I repressed all such hollow feelings of dread, had to repress them. The decent thing to do. As a product of our work ethic. No pain, no gain. Root, hog, or die. So I drove out there. (Still in my VW in those days.)

Our Penitentiary: Can be reached in about twenty minutes by car. Low valley, the village suburban, boring, lots of concrete, several factories, wooded horizon. By the way, you can't say that everyone in our city knows our penitentiary, the four hundred inmates represent barely more than one tenth of one percent of the population. And yet the institution should be familiar to Sunday hikers, even if many of them are more likely to take it for a brewery or an insane asylum. Once you have passed the guarded entryway, however, and are standing in front of the main building, you might almost believe you are standing before an abortive architectural attempt at a church or a chapel of red brick. And the vaguely religious impression stays right with you once you get to the gatekeeper: friendly, gentle faces, à la Salvation Army; a devout silence everywhere, soothing to the nerves, though perhaps somewhat depressing, you automatically yawn in the cool half-light, Justice has assumed her sleepy face, no wonder, really, considering the lady always has her eyes bound. And then there are the other signs of charity and the cure of souls: a bearded priest emerges, busy and unwearied, then the prison chaplain, later a female psychologist, wearing glasses, you can sense that they're out to save souls, to strengthen, to encourage; from the far end of the dismal corridor, however, comes a shimmer of a more menacing world, although the barred glass doors allow no clear view beyond, and the two men in civvies waiting submissive and somber on a bench outside the warden's office likewise awaken some faint mistrust, a vague uneasiness. But once the glass doors are opened, you cross over the mysterious threshold, advance into its innermost region, whether as a slightly embarrassed member of a commission, or as a prisoner, delivered here by Justice herself, you stand in astonishment before a paternal realm of strictest, though not inhumane order, before three mighty five-storied galleries, which can be surveyed from a single point all at once, not gloomy at all, but rather flooded with light from above, before a world of cages and bars, yet not without friendliness and individuality, even from here you can spot through some half-open cell door a ceiling painted sky blue and the gentle green of a potted linden, or there, the amiable, contented figures in their brown institutional garb; the inmates enjoy excellent health, the cloistered, regular mode of life, the early lights-out, the simple diet, all work verifiable wonders; the library offers—in addition to biographies and books of travel, in addition to devotional books of both confessions—if not the latest literature, then the true classics, and the administration provides one film presentation per week, this week *Whiz Kids Like Us*; the percentage of those who attend the sermon substantially exceeds that of the population attending outside these walls; life unwinds slowly and regularly, moderation governs how a man is both kept and entertained, he gets his report card, good behavior pays off, makes conditions easier, though of course only if someone has only a decade or even a few years to serve, in which case the training pays. Whereas in hopeless cases, for those serving life, restrictions are eased without any obligation for self-improvement; such men are in fact the pride of the house: Drossel and Zärtlich, for instance, who, when they were busy at mischief, terrified and alarmed the citizenry, are handled by the guards with timid respect, they are the star prisoners and regard themselves as such. Which is not to deny that, as a result, envy looms up now and then among the ordinary criminals and one of them may, please God, decide that the next time he'll be more thorough about his business; and the medal of honor that our penitentiary received has its reverse side, but taken as a whole, who wouldn't grow virtuous there; broken men, fallen from their high positions and posts, begin to hope anew, cutthroats turn to anthroposophy, erstwhile sex offenders and perpetrators of incest take up intellectual endeavors; paper bags are glued, baskets woven, books bound, brochures printed, members of the federal cabinet even have their suits custom-made in the tailor shop; all the while the warm aroma of bread wafts through the place—the bakery is famous, its sandwich buns a marvel (the cold cuts for them are delivered); parakeets, doves, radios can be earned by hard work and good manners, there are evening schools for continuing education, and, not without some envy, it begins to dawn on you, you suddenly realize, that it is this world, and not ours, that is in order.

Conversation with the Warden: To my surprise I was asked to see Zeller, the warden. He received me in his office, in a room with a respectable conference table, telephone, files. On the walls were bulletin boards, black ones, full of memos, lots of calligraphy—among prisoners, as unfortunately everywhere in our country, there are many teachers. The window had no bars, with a view of the prison walls and a piece of lawn—that, too, would have been schoolyardlike had not absolute silence reigned. Not a car horn, not a sound, like an old folks' home.

The warden greeted me, reserved and cool, and we sat down.

"Herr Spät," he began the conversation, "the prisoner Isaak Kohler has requested that you pay him a visit. I have approved this meeting, and you will speak with Kohler with a guard present."

I knew from Stüssi-Leupin that he was allowed to speak to his clients without witnesses.

"Stüssi-Leupin has our complete trust," the warden said in reply to my question. "By which I don't mean to imply that we don't trust you, but we don't know you yet."

"I understand."

"And there's something else, Herr Spät," the warden continued, somewhat friendlier now. "Before you speak with Kohler, I'd like to share with you my opinion of the prisoner. Perhaps it's something important for you to know. Please don't misunderstand me. It's no business of mine why people are under my supervision here. That's immaterial. My job is to carry out their sentences. That's my only job. And for that reason I shall say nothing about Kohler's crime, but I must admit to you that I am personally confused by the man."

"In what way?" I asked.

The warden hesitated a little before he answered: "The man appears to be completely happy," he then said.

"But that should please you," I suggested.

"Well, yes—I don't know," the warden responded.

"Your operation is after all a model prison," I said.

"I do my best," the warden sighed, "but nevertheless. A multimillionaire sitting happily in his cell, that sounds indecent."

Up on the prison wall, a large fat blackbird was out for a stroll, hoping apparently that he could stay on, having been lured by the twitters, songs, and whistles of the well-tended birds in their cages, whose occasionally overpowering calls could be heard coming from the barred windows. It was a hot day, summer appeared about to flare up again, above the woods clouds were gathering, and from the village came the booming strokes of the steeple clock. Nine o'clock.

I lit a Parisienne. He shoved an ashtray over to me.

"Herr Spät," the warden continued, "imagine a convict who dares to tell you to your face that he finds his prison wonderful, the guards first-rate, that he is perfectly happy and needs nothing else. Incredible. It really disgusted me."

"But why?" I asked. "Aren't your guards first-rate?"

"Of course they are," the warden replied, "but that's for me to say, not the prisoners. People don't shout for joy in hell."

"That's true," I admitted.

"It made me furious and I ordered that the rules be strictly enforced, although the Ministry of Justice has instructed me to be as lenient as possible, and no prison regulations in the world forbid a prisoner to be perfectly happy. But it's made a complete emotional mess of me. Herr Spät, you've got to understand this. Kohler was placed in our customary solitary confinement, cut off from daylight—well, I admit, that's forbidden, actually—but even after a few days I was struck by how the guards took to Kohler, practically revered him."

"And now?" I asked.

"Now I've got used to it," the warden grumbled.

"You revere him as well?"

The warden gave me a thoughtful look. "You see, Herr Spät," he said, "when I sit there in his cell and listen to him—damn it all, a power seems to come from him, a confidence, that could make a man almost believe in humanity, in everything good and beautiful, even our chaplain has been swept away by it, it's like a plague. But thank God I was born a healthy realist and don't believe in people who are perfectly happy. And least of all in the ones in penitentiaries, however much we try to make life easier here with us. We're not beasts, after all. But criminals are criminals. And that's why I tell myself: The man can be dangerous, must be dangerous. You're new at your profession, and so be careful that he doesn't set a trap for you; perhaps you'd best stay out of it entirely. Of course that's just a piece of advice, you're a lawyer after all and can decide for yourself. If only I didn't feel so torn. The man is either a saint or a devil, and I consider it my duty to warn you, which I have done."

"Many thanks, Warden," I said.

"I'll have them get Kohler for you," the warden said with a sigh.

The Job: The conversation with the perfectly happy man took place in an adjoining room. Furniture and view were the same. I stood up as the guard led in Dr.h.c Isaak Kohler. The old man was wearing his brown prison garb; his black-uniformed guard looked like a mail carrier.

"Please, do sit down, Spät," Dr.h.c. Isaak Kohler said, acting very much the host, generous and jovial. Impressed, I thanked him and took my seat. Then I offered the prisoner a Parisienne. Kohler declined it.

"I don't smoke anymore," he declared. "I'm using this opportunity to combine utility with pleasure."

"You find the prison experience to be an especially pleasurable one, Herr Kohler?" I asked.

He gazed at me in surprise: "You don't?"

"I'm not confined to one," I answered.

He beamed. "It's splendid. The peace! And quiet! My previous life was, I grant, a rather grueling one. The trust and all."

"I can well imagine," I concurred.

"And no telephone," he said, "and I've got my health back. Just look." He did several knee bends. "I couldn't do that a month ago," he declared with pride. "We even have a gymnastics club here."

"I know," I said.

The fat blackbird was still walking hopefully around outside, or maybe it was a different one. The perfectly happy man regarded me benevolently. "We ran into each other on a previous occasion," he said.

"I know."

"At the Café Du Théâtre, which has indeed played a certain role in my life. You watched me play billiards."

"I don't understand anything about billiards."

"Still don't?"

"Still don't, Herr Kohler."

The prisoner laughed and turned to his guard: "Möser, would you be so kind as to give our young friend a light?"

The guard leapt up, came over with a lighter.

"Why of course, Herr Deputy, the least I can do." He was beaming too.

Then the guard sat down again. I began to smoke. The cordiality of the two exhausted me. I would have liked to open the large barred windows, but that was probably not allowed in a prison.

"You see, Spät," he said, "I am a simple inmate, nothing more, and Möser is one of my guards. A splendid fellow. He has initiated me in the mysteries of beekeeping. I already feel like a beekeeper, and I'm learning Esperanto from Brunner, another guard—whom I'd like you to meet as well. All our conversations are in that language. You can observe it all for yourself: serenity, coziness, good will everywhere, the profoundest peace. And before? My God!… I'm reading Plato in the original, weaving baskets—do you need a basket, Spät?"

"Sorry, I don't."

"Herr Deputy Kohler's baskets are masterpieces," the guard proudly confirmed from his corner. "I taught him myself how to weave baskets, and now he surpasses all our other basket-weavers. Really, I'm not exaggerating."

I expressed my regrets. "I'm very sorry, I don't need one."

"What a shame, I really would have liked to give you one."

"Kind of you."

"As a memento."

"Can't be helped."

"What a shame. What a rotten shame."

I was growing impatient. "Could you tell me now why you've asked me here?" I inquired.

"Of course," he replied. "The least I can do. I completely forgot that you've come from out there, are in a hurry, caught up in the whirl. So down to business: You told me that evening in the Du Théâtre, perhaps you recall yourself, that you hoped to work for yourself."

"I've got my own practice now."

"So I've been told. How's business?"

"Herr Kohler," I said, "that's hardly to the point here."

"Bad, then." He nodded. "Thought so. And your office is in a garret on Spiegelgasse, correct? That's bad too. Very bad."

I had had enough and stood up. "Either you now inform me what you want of me, Herr Kohler, or I'm leaving," I said bluntly.

The perfectly happy man stood up as well, suddenly taking on an irresistible power, pressed me back down into my chair with both hands, which lay like weights on my shoulders.

"Stay," he commanded menacingly, almost malevolently.

I had no choice but to obey. "As you please," I said, and sat there silent. The guard too.

Kohler sat down again. "You need money," he observed.

"That's not up for discussion here," I answered.

"I'm prepared to offer you a job."

"I'm listening."

"I want you to reinvestigate my case."

I flinched. "Meaning you want to appeal it, Herr Kohler?"

He shook his head. "If I were to pursue an appeal, that would necessarily imply that there is something wrong with my sentence, but there is nothing wrong with it. My life is a closed case, it's been filed away. I know that the warden sometimes thinks I'm a fraud and you, Spät, probably think so too. That's understandable. But I am neither a saint nor a devil, I'm simply a man who's discovered that you don't need anything more to live than a cell, hardly more than you need to die, a bed will do for that, and later a coffin, because man's destiny is contained in thought, not in action. Any jackass can act."

"Fine," I said, "those are laudable principles. But now I'm supposed to act in your stead, to reinvestigate your case. Might this jackass inquire what you're really up to?"

"I'm not up to anything," Dr.h.c. Isaak Kohler answered simply. "I've been thinking. About the world, about humankind, maybe even about God. But I need some material for the task, otherwise my thoughts circle in a vacuum. What I'm asking of you is nothing more than a little help with my studies, which you may simply regard as a millionaire's hobby. Nor are you the only person that I'm asking to lend a helping hand. Do you know old Knulpe?"

"The professor?"

"That's the one."

"I studied under him."

"You see. He's retired now, and just to keep him from vegetating, I've given him a job as well. He's doing a piece of research: the consequences of a murder. He's determining the effects resulting from the somewhat violent demise of his colleague, including the ongoing effects. He's having great fun with it. The idea is to plumb the depths of reality, to measure exactly what effects one deed has. But as far as your task goes, my good man, that's of quite a different nature, set up, in a certain sense, as a counterbalance to Knulpe's work."

"In what sense?"

"You are to reinvestigate my case under the presumption that I was not the murderer."

"I don't understand."

"You are to create a fiction, nothing more."

"But you are, in point of fact, the murderer, and that makes your fiction quite meaningless," I declared.

"That's the only thing that gives it meaning," Kohler answered. "You're not supposed to investigate reality at all—our good old Knulpe is doing that—but rather one of the possibilities behind the reality. You see, my dear Spät, we know very well what reality is, that's why I'm in here weaving baskets, but we hardly know what possibility is. Possibility is something almost limitless, while reality is set within strictest limits, since, after all, only one of all those possibilities can become reality. Reality is only an exception to the rule of possibility, and can therefore be thought of quite differently too. From which follows that we must rethink reality in order to forge ahead into possibility."

I laughed. "A remarkable train of thought, Herr Kohler."

"One gets to pondering lots of things in these parts," he said. "You see, Herr Spät, it often happens during the night, when I'm gazing at stars between the bars in the windows, that I start thinking about how reality might look if, instead of me, someone else had been the murderer. Who would that other person be? I want you to answer those questions for me. I'll pay you a fee of thirty thousand, fifteen thousand in advance."

I said nothing.

"Well?" he asked.

"Sounds like a pact with the devil," I answered.

"I'm not demanding your soul."

"Maybe you are."

"You're risking nothing."

"Possibly. But I don't see the point of this whole business."

He shook his head, laughed.

"It's enough that I see the point. All the rest is no worry of yours. I'm asking nothing of you except that you agree to a proposal that breaks no law and that I need for my research into possibility. I will, needless to say, cover all your expenses. Get in touch with a private detective, Lienhard would be best, pay him whatever he wants, there's money enough, proceed in any fashion you like."

I turned this strange proposal over in my mind again. I didn't like it; I could smell a trap but was unable to discover what it was.

"And why have you turned to me, of all people?" I asked.

"Because you don't know anything about billiards," he answered unruffled.

And with that I made my decision.

"Herr Kohler," I replied, "this job is too fuzzy for me."

"Let my daughter know your definite answer," Kohler said and stood up.

"There's nothing for me to think further about, I'm turning you down," I said and stood up myself.

Kohler gazed at me calmly, beaming, happy, rosy.

"You'll take on this job of mine, my young friend," he said. "I know you better than you know yourself. An opportunity is an opportunity, and you need it. That's all I wanted to say to you. And now, Möser, let's go weave baskets."

They departed, arm in arm, I swear, and I was glad to leave this abode of perfect happiness. In haste. Took to my heels. Determined to keep my distance from all this, never to see Kohler again.

Then I agreed after all. True, I was of a mind to break it off the next morning. I felt my reputation as a lawyer was at stake, even though I had no reputation, but Kohler's proposal was pointless, a bagatelle, beneath the dignity of my profession, simply a foolish way to earn some money and jettison my pride. In those days, I wanted to get through this world neat and clean, yearned for real trials, for the chance to help people. I wrote a letter to the canton deputy informing him yet again of my decision. The matter was finished as far as I was concerned. With the letter in my pocket, I left my room on Freiestrasse, as I did every morning, at nine on the dot, with the intention of going first, as was my custom, to the Select, then later to my studio (the garret on Spiegelgasse), later still to the quay. I greeted my landlady at the door, squinted into the sunlight over toward the mailbox beside the grocery, a few steps, ridiculously few, but since life often functions like a trashy novel, that very morning—that sultry, oppressive workaday morning, ever so typical for our city—between nine and ten, as noted, I met, one right after the other: (a) old man Knulpe, (b) Friedli, the architect, (c) Lienhard, the private detective.

*

(a) Old man Knulpe: He caught me at the mailbox. I was just about to drop in my rejection letter when he moved in ahead of me with a whole bundle of letters, which he carefully dropped in one after the other. As always, the old man was accompanied by his wife. Professor Carl Knulpe was almost six foot six, emaciated, nothing, it seemed, but skin and bones, like Simon Berger, the preacher, and Nicholas of Flüe, but without the beard, unkempt, dirty, wearing a cape, summer and winter, topped by a beret. His spouse was equally tall, equally emaciated, equally unkempt and dirty, and also wore, year round, a cape and a beret, so that many people took her not for his wife but for his twin brother. Both were eminent in their field, both sociologists. Yet however inseparable they were in daily life, they were archenemies in science, doing nasty battle with each other in journals; he was a great Liberal of the old school (*Capitalism, the Intellectual Adventure,* Francke, 1938), she an impassioned Marxist, known under the name Moses Staehelin (*Marxist Humanism in This World,* Europa Publishers, 1939), and both were equally branded by political developments: Carl Knulpe was denied a visa for the US, Moses Staehelin for the USSR; he had made stern pronouncements about "instinctively Marxist tendencies" in the United States, she even more merciless ones about the "petit bourgeois betrayal" of the Soviet Union. Had. Unfortunately the pluperfect is necessary: two weeks ago, a truck belonging to Stürzeler Demolition made purée of them both; he was buried, she cremated, a stipulation in the will that caused considerable difficulty with the funeral.

"Good day," I said, calling attention to myself, the letter to Kohler in hand. Professor Carl Knulpe did not return the greeting, only squinted leerily down at me through his dusty rimless glasses, and his wife (wearing the same sort of glasses) said nothing either.

"I don't know exactly if you still remember me, Herr Professor," I said somewhat crestfallen.

"Course, course I do," Knulpe answered. "Remember. Studied law and knocked about in my sociology classes. Look a little like a professional student. Pass your exams?"

"Long ago, Herr Professor."

"Now a lawyer?"

"Yes indeed, Herr Professor."

"Good work, good work. Socialist, right?"

"Sort of, Herr Professor."

"A valiant slave of the capitalists, right?" Carl Knulpe's wife asked.

"Sort of, Frau Professor."

"Take it have something on your mind," Carl Knulpe observed.

"Indeed I do, Herr Professor."

"Walk with us," she said. I accompanied the two of them. We walked toward Pfauen Square, I still hadn't dropped the letter in the box—my monumental forgetfulness—but there were lots of mailboxes yet.

"Well?" he asked.

"I visited Dr.h.c. Isaak Kohler, Herr Professor. In prison."

"I see, I see. Our merry murderer, merry as a cricket. Ah yes, he summoned you to him as well?"

"Exactly."

First one would ask a question, then the other.

"Is he still as happy as ever?"

"And how!"

"Still simply beaming?"

"Sure is."

We passed another mailbox. Actually I intended to stop there and drop my letter in, but the Knulpes kept on moving, quite unobservant and taking great hasty strides. I had to jog to keep up with them.

"Kohler told me you've accepted a rather peculiar commission, Herr Professor," I said.

"Peculiar? In what way peculiar?"

"Herr Professor! Cross your heart: For Kohler to have someone research the consequences of the murder he committed is really as crazy as can be. Here the fellow commits a murder in broad daylight, with no motive, bold as brass, and then commissions a sociological study of the crime, under the pretext of plumbing the depths of reality."

"And they shall be plumbed, young man. Fathom upon fathom."

"But there must be something behind it! Some devilry or other!" I shouted.

The Knulpes halted. I was panting. He wiped his rimless glasses, moved close to me so that I had to look up at him, he down at me. He put his glasses back on, his eyes glowered. His wife, too, glowering at me with outrage, had edged close to her spouse and so to me as well.

"Science is behind it, young man, only science. For the first time it will be possible to investigate the results of a murder in bourgeois society with methodical thoroughness, to treat it exhaustively. Thanks to our princely murderer. A tremendous opportunity! Connections begin to emerge! Connections of family, profession, politics, finance, culture. Not at all surprising. Everything in this world, and in our beloved city as well, is connected, everyone leans on someone else, advances someone else's cause, and when one falls, others go tumbling as well, and thus many have tumbled. Am in the midst of my account of the consequences at our beloved alma mater. And that's only the beginning."

"Beg your pardon, a car."

I pulled them both to safety. In their excitement the Knulpes had wandered from the sidewalk into the street, and a taxi had to slam on its brakes. It was overfilled, an old lady with a hat full of artificial flowers banged against the windshield, the driver yelled out his window, very crudely. The Knulpes didn't even blanch.

"Totally immaterial," he said, "statistically irrelevant whether we get run over or not. Only the task, only science, counts."

But Frau Professor Knulpe was of a different opinion. "It would have been a pity in my case," she maintained.

The taxi pulled away. Knulpe returned to the topic of his sociological researches.

"Murder is murder, to be sure, but for a scientist it is a phenomenon to be investigated like any other. Up to now, people have limited themselves to determining the causes, motives, background, milieu; my task is to plunge into the consequences. And let me say this: A blessing for our alma mater, a blessing for the whole university, this murder was, one would like to commit murder oneself, so to speak. Yes, of course, regrettable taken by itself, a crime like that, but through the unexpected gap that Winter left behind, fresh air, a fresh spirit, comes streaming in. Amazing, what all becomes clear, our dear departed Winter was sand in the gears, a backward element, as Shakespeare said: 'the Winter of our discontent,' but I intend neither to malign nor make fun of him, will, rather, simply present, deliver the facts, young man, facts and nothing more."

We had arrived at Pfauen Square.

"Godspeed, my good attorney," the Knulpes said and took their leave. "Have an appointment with an important person from the Federal Institute of Technology," he added. "Have to research that terrain now, Winter's influence on the education commission is a chapter to itself, have got wind of scandals. Rosy prospects." At the entrance to the restaurant they turned around again, raised fingers. "Think scientifically, young man, think scientifically. You've still to learn that. Even an attorney must learn it, my good man," Frau Professor Knulpe, alias Moses Staehelin, said.

They disappeared, and I still had not mailed my letter.

(b) Friedli, the architect: Shortly afterward, sat next to him briefly at the Select, the letter still in my pocket. Select: Café, people sit out in front, and sit and sit, have been sitting there for ages, since time immemorial, or at least since millions of years ago, when brontosaurs waded their way downriver. I knew Friedli from my Stüssi-Leupin days; his real-estate speculations ran into trouble now and again, but nothing could slow him down, he was and still is the avalanche of fat that sweeps our city clean, so that in the gaps he leaves behind, new office buildings, condos, apartments, can rise, except that they cost more, with fat rents to match. The natural catastrophe at close range: In his fifties, an enormous bulge of sweating lard, the eyes stuck in somewhere, small and glistening, the nose tiny, the ears too, everything else gigantic, self-made man, a child of Langstrasse (my old lady, dear Spät, hired out as a laundress, my old man drank himself to death, I even poured a bottle of beer into his grave at the burial). Not only a patron of cycling rallies, without whose special purses there would be no six-day races, where he sits enthroned in the stadium, wolfing down countless local sausage specialties, but also a patron of music, thanks to whom our Tonhalle orchestra and our opera house are saved from sinking into absolute mediocrity; who lured Klemperer, Bruno Walter, even Karajan himself, to conduct for us, and who is now advancing Mondschein's career, so that despite his having disfigured our city with his new and renovated buildings, he at least transfigures it again with a little fine art.

He recognized me at once. The warm foehn winds, as noted, were blowing that morning, making everyone feel right at home, lamed and bewitched by our flabby climate, they sat squeezed together; I was glued up against Friedli, who was in the best of moods, dunking one croissant after another in his café au lait, in a glut of lip-smacking, slurping excess, the coffee running in brown streaks down his silk tie and white shirt.

The source of his joy was a death notice in our world-famous local paper. As the result of a tragic accident, it had pleased God to call unto Himself "our never-to-be-forgotten husband, father, son, brother, uncle, son-in-law, and brother-in-law, Otto Erich Kugler. His life was purest love."

"An enemy of yours?" I asked.

"A friend."

I offered my condolences.

"Just had to go roaring off to Cham and into a tree, good, honest, dear old Kugler," Friedli explained, beaming, slurping coffee, dunking croissants and eating, "rolling off into life eternal."

"I'm sorry to hear it," I said.

"You should have seen his Fiat, just a tangle of tin."

"Dreadful."

"Fate. We all have to die sometime."

"Apparently," I said.

"Hell," he said, "you don't seem to have any notion what this stroke of fate means for little old me, do you?"

I didn't. Massive little old him held me in his friendly gawking gaze.

"Kugler leaves a widow behind," he declared, "a splendid female."

It suddenly dawned on me. "And now you want to marry this splendid female."

Friedli the architect shook that portion of fat where one presumed his head might be. "No, young man, I don't want to marry the widow, but the wife of her lover. Another female deluxe. Got it? Quite simple: If the lover wants to marry the widow, he's got to get divorced first, and then I'll marry his wife."

"Social mathematics," I said.

"Got it."

"But then you'll have to get divorced too," I reminded him, in the vague hope of picking up some business.

"I am. Have been for a week. My fifth divorce."

Silence again.

The waiter brought fresh croissants. A school class crossed the square, girls, several in pigtails, some of them already young women. One bevy halted to look at movie stills. Friedli ogled them.

"You're the strange lawyer with an office in a garret on Spiegelgasse, aren't you?" he asked, watching the girls.

I had to admit it.

"It's nine-thirty," he observed, grinned and turned back to me. "I don't want to be indiscreet, I'm really a well-mannered fellow, Spät, but I have the distinct feeling that you've not been to your office yet this morning."

"You guessed it," I said, "your distinct feeling is not in error. I'll make it over there in an hour maybe, or this afternoon sometime."

"I see. Maybe this afternoon." He regarded me thoughtfully. "Dear Spät," he said, "I spent the morning tromping around a construction site from seven till ten before nine," he said modestly. "I earn millions. Fine. With my buildings, with my speculations. Neat and proper. But that takes work, discipline, damn it. I drink like a fish, I admit, but pull myself together again every morning."

The colossus of lard laid a paternal arm over my shoulders. "My dear Spät," he continued gently, all fat gigantic emotion, glistening with the steam rising from his coffee, croissant crumbs on his face and hands, "my dear Spät, I'm going to be straight with you. You're having some real difficulties getting started, don't try to pretend with me. And the result: You don't count as a serious man at all. A lawyer who isn't sitting behind his desk by nine-thirty is no more than thin air to a reputable business man. I don't want to press all that hard, you don't look like a loafer to me, but so far you've never been able to get up the nerve for a real breakneck leap into the bustle of life. And do you know why? Because you don't know how to cut a figure, don't have the guts or the spine for it. University studies are fine and dandy, but good grades don't impress anyone but the schoolmasters. A desk isn't enough, you can sit there on your throne as long as you like, the clients won't come swarming in. No sir, and why should they? No, my friend, your disappointment is uncalled for. VWs and garrets aren't just symbols of social poverty but of a certain intellectual poverty also, no offense intended. Honesty and modesty are fine enough, but a lawyer has to step up and make the earth tremble. The first thing you need is a real office suite; you'll get nowhere with that pigeon cote of yours, nobody is going to come climbing up there behind you. After all, people want to sue, not do feats of athletic derring-do. In a word, it can't go on like this. I'd like to give you a chance. Come see me at my office tomorrow morning at seven, bring along a mere four thousand, and then we'll see you get set up in a decent space on Zeltweg."

(What followed was a lengthy expatiation upon a gigantic real-estate deal, plus further consumption of croissants and café au lait, the expatiation ironic and sardonic, delivered in the knowledge that in these parts the biggest swindles must be managed, get managed, legally; and then he came around to a Stravinsky festival and a Honegger cycle, and as I got up, he expressed his opinion that the reason the traffic was so chaotic was that our mayor was a pedestrian.)

*

(c) Fredi Lienhard, private detective: Same age as I. Gaunt, black-haired, a man of conspicuous taciturnity and short sentences. Only child of divorced parents. As a high school student he was suspected of having murdered his mother along with her lover, they were both naked in Mama's bedroom, stretched out nice and proper, she on the bed, the lover, her psychiatrist, from Küsnacht, in front of it, like a throw rug. Lienhard was called out of his final exams; he was just about to translate a passage of Tacitus when the police nabbed him; his situation looked hopeless, he was the sole suspect, only he had been in the house on the night of the murder, although, according to his testimony, he had spent it peacefully on the top floor in his teenage pad stuffed with the classics and zoology books. It was his additional bad luck to have just turned eighteen, so that he ended up not in the clutches of the juvenile authorities but in the considerably less merciful clutches of Jämmerlin. The interrogations, during his custody and later before the jury, were carried out with some rigor, too, with Jämmerlin assaulting the high school boy with every trick in the book, but Lienhard held up magnificently, an absolute master; the solid evidence suddenly turned out to contain serious contradictions, and finally there was no choice but to acquit him; there weren't even legal dodges enough to place him under a guardian. Jämmerlin raged, suffered his first nervous breakdown, attempted several appeals, vain ones however, to the Supreme Court to have the case reopened—all the more eagerly since Lienhard began to take his revenge. The suspect had come into money, mad sums; his divorced father had been rich as Croesus and bequeathed it all to him, and then there was the capital from his well-financed mother, so that the dough rolled in, gushed in, flew in from all sides, piled up, added up, multiplied, squared, cubed; he stashed away one inheritance after another within a very short space of time—grandparents, aunts, uncles, as well as any heirs they might have had, shoved hastily off, thronged their way, so to speak, into eternity; it was as if heaven and hell were employing their full lethal resources in order to bless Lienhard with the world's wealth, and blessed he was. Having just been released from Jämmerlin's domain and not yet twenty years old, he emerged a multimillionaire. It was fabulous, involving more luck than brains, though there was plenty of the latter. For he proceeded to attack the prosecutor by means as systematic as they were simple: He never left his side. Jämmerlin could not go anywhere without crossing paths with Lienhard. At every summation before a jury, there would be Lienhard's face grinning at him from somewhere in the room. If he was dining at a restaurant, Lienhard would be at the next table. He was always close at hand. Wherever Jämmerlin took up residence, Lienhard would be living next door, if Jämmerlin angrily moved to a rented apartment, suddenly there was Lienhard rooming above him. Jämmerlin was at the end of his tether. The sight of Lienhard was unbearable. Several times he came close to throwing himself at him, to using violence, and once he even bought himself a revolver. He moved from one street to another, from one neighborhood to another, from Hinterbergstrasse to C. F. Meyer Strasse, from Wollishofen to Schwamendingen; finally, leaving civilization behind, he built himself a chalet on Katzenschwanzstrasse, near Witikon, and when someone started building on the next lot, Jämmerlin smelled a rat. It turned out that the builder was the vice-president of a bank, but he was only temporarily pacified. And rightly so, for the next spring, as he stood in his shirt-sleeves watering his new lawn, there beside the freshly painted garden fence stood Lienhard waving jovially his way, acting as if they were old acquaintances (which in fact they were), and introducing himself as the new neighbor. The bank vice-president had been a straw man. Jämmerlin staggered back toward his house, barely making it to the porch. Second nervous breakdown, plus heart attack. The doctors wavered—madhouse or hospital? Jämmerlin lay at home in bed, immobile, waxen, was presumed finished. But he was tough. He pulled himself together, though the inner man was a shambles. As far as Lienhard went, silent surrender. The two continued to live side by side. At the edge of the woods. With a view of Witikon. Jämmerlin did not dare budge again. All the more so since he was also powerless against another one of Lienhard's activities. Lienhard had become a private detective, doing business on a grand scale. He had rented space in one of the sumptuous office buildings on Talacker, took a whole floor, you floated from one room to another. Behind modern office desks sat several weighty gentlemen with close-cropped hair, old athletes, though beer-bellied now, contentedly smoking cigars, and former police officers that he had bought up—the financial terms Lienhard could offer appreciably surpassed anything the city might pay. But it was not their being hired that annoyed Jämmerlin, business was business, no complaint could be raised there, unfortunately. What tormented him was quite different acquisitions.

You could not miss the fact that these elegant rooms on Talacker were often rife with the very elements of society that Jämmerlin had once brought to judgment, with former convicts and toughs, who, switching over to honest work, were now employed as experts in their field. Lienhard's "criminal division" also had great success in our city, despite the horrendous fees he was accustomed to charging and the juicy expense accounts he toted up, because Lienhard's Private Inquiries, as it was officially called, delivered proof of the infidelity or innocence of suspected spouses, came up with fathers when they chose not to place themselves automatically at the mothers' disposal, provided information, both private and industrial, had people watched, followed, dug up, made discreet arrangements—and was used by people in the prosecutor's office to frustrate some of Jämmerlin's plans, to deliver counterevidence, even to come up with new evidence altogether. Many a trial took a happy and unexpected turn in the accused's favor thanks to Lienhard's office; moreover, lawyers would meet secretly here on Talacker, Lienhard was a brilliant host, even political opponents exchanged business cards at his place.

All this as preamble. Our meeting that morning took place directly in front of the Select, shortly after ten; Friedli had finally departed, and I too had got up with the intention of mailing the letter to Kohler, though admittedly I was no longer quite so firm in my resolve, and up came Lienhard, or more precisely, up drove Lienhard. In a Porsche. He stopped. He knew me from my student days, had studied law himself, though only for one semester, had at one time made me an offer to join up with him, but I had declined.

"Lawyer," he said, without looking at me from the wheel of his open Porsche, "something for me?"

"Possibly," I answered.

"Climb in," he ordered.

I obeyed.

"Fast car," I observed.

"Five thousand," Lienhard remarked, meaning that he'd be willing to sell the Porsche for that amount. He owned a lot of cars; sometimes it seemed as if he drove a different one every day.

Then I told him about my meeting with old Kohler. Lienhard drove along the lake, as was his custom—he transacted his more important deals in his car. "No witnesses," he once explained. He drove at a steady speed, careful to a fault, and listened attentively. When I had finished, he came to a stop. In Uetikon. In front of a telephone booth.

"Lucrative," he declared. "Investigation?"

I nodded. "If I accept."

He entered the telephone booth, and when he returned he suggested, "His daughter's at home."

Then we drove to Weinbergstrasse, parked in front of Kohler's villa.

"Go on in," Lienhard ordered.

I pulled up short. "I'm supposed to accept the job?"

"Of course."

"Too obscure," I offered for his consideration.

He lit a cigarette. "If you don't take the job, someone else will," he replied, and it was as if he had delivered an oration.

I got out. Next to the large entrance, a shiny yellow public mailbox was attached to the wrought-iron fence. As a warning.

My rejection letter was still in my pocket. I knew what my duty was. But why should I turn down Kohler's offer, really, why play the man of character? I needed the money, that was that! It wasn't lying in the streets, some opportunity had to come along, and here it was. I had to cut a figure if I wanted to be a successful lawyer. Friedli, the architect, was right, and I wanted to be successful. And besides, Kohler's job was essentially quite harmless, more a scientific undertaking, he could afford such extravagances.

"You want five thousand for the Porsche?"

"Four," Lienhard answered.

"Generous of you."

"Depends on whether you hire me."

"You don't need the business."

"Would be fun."

"First I want to talk with Kohler's daughter," I said.

"I'll wait," Lienhard answered.

Deposition for the Prosecutor: It can no longer be avoided. I must now take up the subject of my first meeting with Hélène. A painful task, to be dared with caution—yet unavoidable. Even if private matters have to be discussed. Finally, for you will read it with interest and make your underlinings. You: quite right, it's you I mean, Prosecutor Joachim Feuser. Just go ahead and wince yourself awake. Why not get personal here; as Jämmerlin's successor you'll be the second person to read these lines, right after the commandant—are in fact reading them right now—while at the moment I am having one hell of a good time—presumably in both senses of that phrase—greeting you, as it were, from the world beyond. To be frank: You are a pedantic member of your species, even if in contradistinction to our dear departed Jämmerlin you pretend to be so very progressive and run off to all those psychological conferences. You love supporting documents. As per regulation, you've just visited me at the morgue, in your pale raincoat, your hat courteously in your hand and your countenance officially somber. The suicide was done with dispatch, that you must admit, but I've also done a workmanlike job with Kohler, it does look so impressive, the two of us side by side. But now to return from your present, which lies in the future for me, to my own present, which is *your* past. How time overlaps. Got it? Suppose not. At best, annoyed. I've prepared things so carefully.

First, Matters Historical, Architectural, Philosophical: The important events in one's interior life demand a precise framework. In a historical sense as well. And so I've gathered precise information about Kohler's villa. I even did some research in the main library. The building turned out to be the former residence of Nikodemus Molch. Nikodemus Molch, a thinker at the dawn of the twentieth century, bearded like Moses, a European of uncertain ancestry and uncertain nationality (according to one source, the illegitimate son of Alexander III and an Australian songstress; according to another, in reality one Jakob Hager from Burgdorf, a high school teacher previously convicted of sexual assaults on children), ran a free academy financed by rich widows and aesthetically inclined colonels, corresponded with the aged Tolstoy, with the middle-aged Rabindranath Tagore, and the young Klages, planned a movement of cosmic renewal, proclaimed a vegetarian world government, whose decree unfortunately no one obeyed (the First World War, Hitler—although a vegetarian—the Second World War, the whole subsequent mess in fact would have been avoided!), published magazines, dealing partly with the occult, partly with highbrow pornography, wrote mystery plays, converted to Buddhism, and later ended up, though involved in countless bankruptcy and paternity suits and with warrants out for his arrest, as the secretary to the Dalai Lama, reputedly, since several of our fellow countrymen, members of a film team, claimed to have recognized him as the piano player in a Shanghai bar in the thirties.

The Site of the Villa: For a lawyer who came from a poor background, or better, from no background at all, a lawyer who had just decided to dare the breakneck leap (quoting Friedli) into a more pleasant life, the path from Lienhard's Porsche to the front door of Dr.h.c. Isaak Kohler's residence proved quite stimulating; it led through a park. Nature herself was redolent of wealth. The flora was anything but shabby. The trees downright majestic, still in summer glory. Nor did the foehn wind make itself noticeable; even in that regard some sort of agreement must have been reached with the appropriate authorities—many things are possible for the rich. (For nonlocals: by "foehn," we mean a climatic condition in our city that fosters headaches, suicides, adulteries, traffic accidents, and acts of violence.) You walked along a carefully laid-out and weeded gravel path. It was not in any sense a modern park. Laid out more in the old, soigné fashion. Ingeniously trimmed hedges and bushes. Moss-covered statues. Naked, bearded gods with youthful rear ends and calves. Quiet ponds. A pompous pair of peafowl. And yet this park lay in the midst of the city; a single square yard had to be worth astronomical sums. Streetcars thundered all round it, cars sped around it, traffic surged, raged, ting-a-linged and honked like an ocean against the venerable golden-tipped wrought-iron fence, and yet in Kohler's park silence reigned. Presumably the sound waves had been forbidden entry. Only a few birds could be heard.

The House Itself: In reality it had once been a horror, an architectural sink of iniquity designed by the occidental thinker himself. How the canton deputy had managed to make something human, something liveable of it remains one of his secrets. Apparently, cupolas, turrets, oriels, putti, and zodiacal beasts galore (Nikodemus Molch also dabbled in astrology) had been pulled down, the chaos peeled away to reveal a much cozier villa—still heavily gabled, but entwined now with wild grape, ivy, honeysuckle, and roses—large and roomy, and the interior offered me the same effect when, with a last glance at the Porsche, visible only as a red dot, I entered. The architects had done a clever piece of work, knocked down walls, laid wall-to-wall carpet, etc., everything looked comfortable and light. Antique furniture, all of it priceless, famous impressionists on the walls, and later I saw Old Dutch masters (a maid led the way). I was left to wait in the deputy's study. The room was spacious, gilded by the sun. Through the open French doors you could walk directly into the park; the two windows flanking the door went almost to the costly parquet floor. A giant desk, deep leather armchairs, no pictures on the walls here, just books to the ceiling, every one of them a volume on mathematics or natural science, a considerable library, but in rather strange contrast to the billiard table.

This was set back in a broad alcove. Three balls still lay on its green surface, and on the alcove wall was a collection of cues. A great many old ones, with inscriptions. One cue had belonged to Honoré de Balzac, another to Gottfried Keller, another to General Dufour, one to Bismarck, and there was even one said to have been Napoleon's. I looked about me in some embarrassment. The old Dr.h.c.'s presence could be felt everywhere, I felt as if at any moment he might come in from the park, as if I could hear his laugh, feel his attentive gaze brush over me.

The Vision: And then something remarkable happened, something ghostly, really. All at once, I understood the canton deputy. Unexpectedly. The insight more or less attacked me. I suddenly guessed the motive for his actions. I caught its scent from the expensive furniture, from the books, from the billiard table. I detected it in the combination of strictest logic and play that had left its mark on this room. I had forced my way into his lair, and now I saw it clearly. Kohler had not murdered because he was a player of games. He was not a risk-taker. The stakes did not lure him. What lured him was the game itself, the rolling of the balls, the calculation and the execution, the possibility each game presented. Good luck meant nothing to him (which was why he could regard himself as perfectly happy, he wasn't even shamming). He was simply proud of the fact that it lay within his power to choose the rules of the game, loved to follow the unraveling of a necessity that he had himself created—here lay the humor for him. Naturally there were reasons behind all this too. The most sublime instinct for power, perhaps, the mania to play not just with balls but with human beings, the seduction of equating himself with

God. Possible. But not important. As a lawyer I have to remain on the surface of things, not sink down into psychology or, worse, plummet into philosophy or theology. By committing a murder, Kohler had begun a new game, that was all. It was now proceeding according to plan. I was nothing more than one of his billiard balls set in motion by his shot. His actions were perfectly logical. He had not given any motive in court because that had been impossible.

Murderers generally act out of sturdy motives. For hunger or for love. Intellectual motives are rare and then only in some distorted form that has been shaped by politics. Religious motives hardly ever occur and lead directly to the insane asylum. The canton deputy, however, had acted out of a scientific motive. That seems absurd. But he was a thinker. His motives were not concrete but abstract. You had to grab hold of him right there. He loved billiards not as a game for itself but because it served him as a model of reality. As one of its possible simplifications ("model of reality"—I am using a term Mock, the sculptor, loves to use, who spends a lot of his time with physics and little with sculpturing, a muddled loony, whose studio I've been visiting often lately—where can you sit and drink after midnight in this country?—with whom conversation is only barely possible on account of his deafness, but who has turned on a good many lights for me). Kohler busied himself with natural science and mathematics for the same reason. They, too, offered him "models of reality." Except that these models were not enough for him, he had to move on to murder in order to create a new "model." He was experimenting by using a crime, murder was merely a method. That explained his commission to have Knulpe identify the results of the murder, and that explained as well his grotesque commission to have me find other "possible" murderers. Only now, here in his study, alone with the objects the old man occupied himself with, did I understand the conversation I had had with him in the prison. "The idea is to plumb the depths of reality, to measure exactly what effects one deed has" and "We must rethink reality in order to forge ahead into possibility." The Dr.h.c. had shown his hand to me, but I had not understood the game he was playing. Only when you took this game seriously did his motive become evident: He had killed in order to observe, murdered in order to examine, the laws upon which human society is based. Had he admitted this motive in court, however, it would have been regarded as nothing more than an evasion. Such a motive was too abstract for our system of justice. But that is simply the way scientific thought is constructed. Its abstract quality is its shield. But suddenly it can break out of its sheltered existence and become dangerous. Unquestionably, something of the sort had happened with Kohler's experiment: A scientific mind was bent upon murder. By which I mean neither to acquit the deputy nor to attack science. The more intellectual the motive for an act of violence, the more evil it is; the more consciously it is carried out, the less it can be excused. It becomes inhumane. Blasphemous. To that extent, I saw things correctly at that moment, in that regard my vision has been confirmed. It prevented me from admiring Kohler and from ever regarding him as innocent. It helped me to despise him. The certainty that he was the murderer would never leave me from that hour on. It is regrettable, however, that at the time I did not recognize the danger of the game Kohler was continuing to play with my help. I believed that playing along was nothing more than a harmless technical matter, with no consequences. I imagined the game would be played in an empty room, solely in the mind of a blasphemous man. His game had begun with a murder. Why did I not realize at that point that it would inevitably lead to a second murder, to a murder that would have to be committed not by the Dr.h.c. but by us, the representatives of the system of justice with which the old man was playing?

Second, Matters Psychological: A momentous meeting not only demands a detailed physical space but also requires that its reporter be in an appropriate frame of mind. Therefore drank and whored prodigiously. For starters I drank several liters of applejack, bad style, I know (question of price), but I was just drinking to get rolling, and when the girl showed up, I switched to cognac. Not to worry, I've always had a cast-iron stomach. By the way, the girl was not Giselle (the one with the remarkable figure), but Monika (or Marie or Marianne, her name began with *M* at any rate), we had a high time, later she started singing a lot of folk songs from German films, I fell asleep; later still, she had disappeared with my cash. I had moved on to pear brandy in the meantime and I found her near the Bellevue in a café that doesn't serve alcohol. When I stumbled on her, she was with Giselle and her protector (the previously mentioned Lucky), who turned out to be her protector as well. I confronted her, and he was decent enough to set financial matters right, Marlene (or Monika or Magdalena) had to fork it over. We all got along decently for the most part. Grandly, in fact, the waitress overlooked the bottle of Williamine I had brought along, all four of us drank it. Then Hélène arrived, quite unexpectedly, out of the blue, like a vision from another world. From a worse world. Since seeing her with Stüssi-Leupin—when was that, two months ago, three, maybe six?—I hadn't thought of her, or just once, one night when Giselle was enthroned naked above me like a swaying Buddha, but never after that, I'm sure not—or only fleetingly, as I was crossing the rain-drenched street near the Bellevue, but that doesn't count, was simply the effect of the sudden change in weather on my general mood—and now there she stood, she had to have been looking for me in the café, I'm certain. I had to laugh, everybody laughed. Hélène remained calm, friendly, lofty, serene, all the flawless comportment you could ask for, that was the hell of it, that she was always in command of herself, remained calm, friendly, lofty, serene, I could have killed, murdered, strangled, raped her, turned her into a whore, that's what I would have loved to do.

"May I have a word with you, Herr Spät?" she said and gave me an imploring look.

"What kind of a girl is that?" Giselle asked.

"A refined girl," I declared, "a girl from a good family, the precious daughter of a murderer."

"Who does she sleep with?" Marianne (or Magdalena or Madeleine) wanted to know.

"She goes to bed with a top lawyer," I explained, "with the juridical star of stars, with an educated gallows bird, with the grand champion attorney, Stüssi-Leupin, every fuck is an act of jurisprudence."

"Herr Spät," Hélène said.

"Have a seat," I replied. "Would you like to sit on the lap of the famous Lucky, the gentleman who protects these two ladies and whose lawyer I have the honor to be, or would you prefer a chair?"

"A chair," Hélène answered softly.

Lucky shoved a chair her way, politely, stylishly, our perfect man-of-the-world Lucky, with his black moustache, his palmolive face, and apostolical brown eyes, even bowed to her, you could smell his perfume and Camels a mile away. She sat down tentatively. "Actually I wanted to speak with you alone," she said.

"Not necessary." I laughed. "We have no secrets here. I've been sleeping with Miss Giselle for weeks now, and just tonight I slept with our doughty Monika here, or Marianne, or whatever the hell her name is. You see, things are all out in the open. So then, shoot."

Hélène had tears in her eyes.

"You once asked me a question."

"I know."

"As I was having coffee with Herr Stüssi-Leupin—"

"It's perfectly evident what you mean," I interrupted, "you don't have to add a Herr to the bastard's name."

"At the time, I didn't understand the meaning of your question," she said softly.

All at once it had turned quiet. Giselle had slid off my lap, was fixing her makeup. I was furious, guzzled my Williamine, suddenly noticed that my hair was sticking to my head, my face sweaty, my eyes burning, that I hadn't shaved, that I stank, the sudden embarrassment of the two girls annoyed me no end, it was as if they felt ashamed in Hélène's presence, as if a Salvation Army ambience was taking over, I could have smashed the whole place up, the world had gone topsy-turvy. Hélène should have been the one to crawl before these girls, and crawl she would. I kept drinking more Williamine, without saying a word, simply staring into the big dark eyes of the quiet face in front of me.

"Fräulein Hélène Kohler," I said thickly, standing up, ceremoniously, swaying, but I managed it. "Fräulein Hélène Kohler, I would like to file a general statement—yes indeed, file it, that's the right word. I met you, Hélène Kohler, in the company of your bedfellow—quiet, ladies—your bedfellow Stüssi-Leupin. Correct. I asked you whether on the day of the murder you had been the stewardess on the very same flight that was to return the English minister to his wretched little island. Correct, correct, correct. You replied in the affirmative. And now for the decisive point, which I would like to fling in your face—yes, fling it, with all my might, Hélène Kohler. There was a revolver in the Englishman's coat. You took possession of that revolver, easy enough for a stewardess to do, and that revolver was the weapon of your esteemed papa, the murder weapon that was never found, of which you are well aware. You are an accomplice, Hélène Kohler, not just the daughter of a murderer, but a murderer yourself. I loathe you, Hélène Kohler, I can't stand the smell of you, because you stink of murder just like your bastard of a father and not just of schnapps and whores like me. May your body slowly rot away, may cancer devour your esteemed womb, because if you were ever to give birth to a little Stüssi-Leupin, it'd be all over with this world of ours, it's too fragile to handle a monster like that. What a pity that would be for this world, despite all its sins, a pity for these beautiful whores, whom you can't hold a candle to, madame, who ply an honest trade and not a murderous one, my own dear darling, and now would you kindly beat it, scram. Go stretch out under your star lawyer…"

She left. I'm not all that clear about what happened next. I stumbled, I think, at any rate I found myself lying tummy-down on the floor, I think maybe a table was turned over, the bottle of Williamine was emptied (that I'm sure of), a guest with an egghead brow and glasses complained, the woman who ran the place came sailing over, a regular mama to her whores, the noble Lucky helped me to the toilet, I suddenly didn't like his moustache, started hitting him, he had once been an amateur boxer, there was blood, I ended up lying in the urinal, it was unpleasant, especially because it came so thickly smeared with symbolism, like some B movie, all at once the police arrived, Sergeant Stuber and two of his men. They took me down to the precinct for a couple of hours. Interrogation, statement, etc.

Postscript: Let it be noted that, in a purely technical sense, my attempt to describe my first meeting with Hélène has failed. I described my last meeting with her. Therefore, in the future certain precautions are to be taken. Writing in an alcoholic stupor requires a cautious style. Short sentences. Subordinate clauses can prove dangerous. Syntax sows confusion. Plus there is an epilogue for the record (just received another postcard from Kohler, this time from Rio de Janeiro, best wishes, says he's flying from there to San Francisco, then on to Hawaii, then Samoa, so I've got time). To wit: the commandant of the canton police paid me a visit. The visit was important.

Of that I am sure. It's probably also the reason for my being completely sober now. There is no proof of it, but my hunch is that the commandant suspects what I'm up to. That would make things difficult. Arguing against it is the fact that he left the revolver with me. He came quite unexpectedly, around ten, two days after the unfortunate scene in the café. The streets were slushy. Suddenly he was standing in my garret. Down below the sect exulted: "Good Christian man, prepare thy soul, for on the Judgment Day, be sure you've kept it pure and whole, His bolts shall light His way." The commandant was somewhat ill at ease. He glanced in embarrassment across to my desk with its pile of paper full of scribbles.

"Let's hope you don't want to be a writer, too," he growled.

"Why not, Commandant, when you've got something to write about?" I answered.

"Sounds like a threat."

"Take it however you like."

He looked around him, a bottle under his arm. On my couch lay some girl or other. I didn't know her, she had just tagged along, maybe a present from Lucky, had apparently undressed and stretched out, out of some misconception of professionalism (the work ethic makes itself evident everywhere in our country). It had made no difference to me whatever, I had set myself to work; pulled out my papers.

"Get dressed," he ordered. "You'll catch cold if you don't. And then I want to have a word with the lawyer here."

He put the bottle on the table.

"Cognac," he said. "Adet. A rare brand. From a friend in western Switzerland. Wanted to give it a try. Get us two glasses, Spät. She's not drinking any more today."

"Yes sir, Herr Commandant," said the girl.

"Go on home. Your workday is over."

"Yes sir, Herr Commandant."

She was almost dressed now. He looked at her calmly.

"Good night."

"Good night, Herr Commandant."

The girl left. We heard her hurrying down the stairs.

"You know her?" I asked.

"I know her," the commandant replied.

Downstairs the sect was still singing its end-of-the-world chorale: "The sun explodes with dreadful might, the earth doth pass away. Oh, cling in such a dreadful plight, to Jesus Christ, thy stay."

The commandant poured. "To your health."

"To your health."

"Do you own a revolver?" he asked.

There was no point in lying. I took it out of the desk drawer. He examined it, gave it back to me. "You still think Kohler is guilty, don't you?"

"Don't you?"

"Maybe," he answered and sat down on the couch.

"Then why are you giving up the game?" I asked him.

He looked at me.

"So you still intend to win it?"

"In my own way."

He looked at the revolver. I took care of it.

"That's your business," he said, poured another round. "Well, how do you like the Adet?"

"Splendid."

"I'll leave the bottle here with you?"

"Kind of you."

From below a sermon or maybe a prayer could now be heard. "You see, Spät," the commandant said, "you've got yourself in a somewhat unfortunate situation. I don't want to say anything against the honorable Mr. Lucky, still less against that poor thing that just left, on the whole it's not the fault of those two that these things exist, but how far you're going to get as a lawyer for whores is another matter. The review board is going to have to initiate proceedings against you soon, that ought to be clear to you. They have nothing against a lawyer for lowlifes if he makes money, but no use at all for one who doesn't. Their professional honor rebels at that."

"So what?"

"You just asked me a moment ago why I've given up the game, Spät," the commandant continued, lighting one of his fat Bahianos, carefully, without the least tremble. "I'll admit to you that I also consider Kohler guilty and everything that's happened is a farce I would gladly have prevented. But I have no evidence. Have you gotten any further in the matter?"

"No," I said.

"You really haven't?" he asked again.

I said no a second time.

"You don't trust me, do you?" he asked.

"I don't trust anyone."

"Fine," he said. "As you please. The Kohler affair is finished, as far as I'm concerned, it ended with my defeat. Lots of affairs have ended that way for me. Sad to say, but in my profession a man has to be able to swallow defeat. And in yours too, I think. You should pull yourself together, Spät, start fresh."

"That's no longer possible," I replied.

Down below the exultation continued: "The gates of hell shall slam behind, the flames still burning high, 'twill be too late, O humankind, this world is gone for aye."

All at once I was suspicious: "Are you perhaps keeping something from me, Commandant?"

He smoked, looked at me, smoked some more, got up.

"What a pity," he replied and held his hand out to me. "Farewell. Perhaps I'll still have to issue you a professional summons someday."

"Farewell, Herr Commandant," I said.

The Beginning of Love: Here I am at a standstill again. I know there can be no further evasions. I have to find a way to talk about my first meeting with Hélène. I have to admit that I loved Hélène. And, I must add, from the start. Which means since our first meeting. It's hard to confess this, and only now do I feel capable of it. And yet, that love has become impossible. I must therefore give an account of a love that I did not admit to myself when I might possibly have made it work, and that can no longer be made to work. That isn't easy. Of course now I know that Hélène was not what I first saw in her. Only now do I see her as she is. She shares the guilt. Of course I understand her. It's only human for her to cover for her inhuman father. It's unthinkable to demand that she betray her father. Her confession alone could destroy the canton deputy. But she will never make that confession. I am enough of a lawyer, after all, not to exact such a demand. I have to go my own way, she may go hers, but I cannot deny the image I once formed of her. That she does not fit that image, never fitted it, is not her fault. I am sorry for my impetuous words. I know the way I acted was childish. Likewise my catting around and my drinking. She has every right to be what she is, and I have assumed the right to murder her father at some point. Had I got to her father at the airport that night, he would be dead now and so would I. The affair would now be put right, and the world would long since have moved on to its agenda. My life has only one purpose: to settle accounts with Kohler. That settlement will be easy. One shot will suffice. But for now I have to wait. I hadn't included that in my calculations. Nor what it costs me in nerves. Executing justice is something different from having to live in the expectation of executing it. I feel like some frenzied madman. My drinking like this is simply an expression of my absurd position; it's as if I were drunk on justice. The feeling of being in the right is destroying me. Nothing is more horrifying than this feeling. I am executing myself, because I cannot execute old man Kohler. In my frenzy, I can see me and Hélène, I look back at our first meeting. I know that I've lost everything. Nothing can replace happiness. Even when that happiness turns out to be madness, and my madness today is, in reality, sobriety. Unmerciful awareness of the real world. So I think back with sadness. I would like to forget and am incapable of it. It all sticks so clearly in my memory, as if it had just happened. I still hear the tone of her voice, still see her glances, her movements, her dress. And I see myself as well. We were both young. Brand-new. It was less than a year and a half ago. Now I am old, ancient. We showed each other our trust. When it would have been perfectly natural for her to have distrusted me. She must have seen in me nothing but a lawyer who wanted money. But she trusted me from the start. I sensed it that day, and I trusted her as well. I was ready to help her. It was lovely. Even when we were just sitting across from each other, even when we were just talking about practical matters. Naturally I know it was not that way, that it was all a sham, a dream, an illusion, or even worse, a rotten trick that Hélène was playing on me, me of all people, but back then, back then, when I still didn't know, didn't have the faintest suspicion, I was happy.

"Do sit down, Herr Spät," she said. I thanked her. She had taken her seat in a deep leather armchair. I sat down across from her. In another deep leather armchair. It was all somehow remarkable, the girl, maybe twenty-two, tanned, smiling, relaxed and yet hesitant, all the books, the heavy desk, the billiard table and its balls in the background, the rays of sun streaming in, the park behind the half-open glass doors through which Hélène had come. With an elderly gentleman by the name of Förder. He was impeccably dressed, was introduced as Kohler's private secretary, had mutely, almost menacingly, taken my measure. Then he left, without saying goodbye, without having said so much as a single word. Now that we were alone, Hélène was ill at ease. So was I. The vision of her father had lamed me, left me unable to speak. I felt sorry for her. I realized that she would never understand her father, that she suffered because his actions were so incomprehensible.

"Herr Spät," she said, "my father has always talked about you a lot."

That surprised me. I looked at her in astonishment. "Always?"

"Ever since he met you in the Du Théâtre."

"And what did he say about me?" I asked.

"He was worried about your practice," she answered.

"I didn't have one yet at the time," I replied.

"But you have one now," she observed.

"It's not exactly successful," I admitted.

"He has informed me about the job he's asked you to do," Hélène continued.

"I know," I replied.

"And you accept?"

"I've decided to."

"I've been filled in on the conditions," she said. "Here is a check for the advance. Fifteen thousand. And another ten thousand for expenses."

Hélène handed me the check. I took it, folding the paper once over.

"Your father is generous," I said.

"It's very important to him that you carry out his commission," she declared.

"I'll try my level best."

I slipped the check into my wallet. We fell silent. She was no longer smiling. I sensed that she was searching for words.

"Herr Spät," she falteringly said at last, "I am aware that the commission you've undertaken is a strange one."

"Rather."

"Herr Förder thinks it strange too."

"I can believe that."

"But it must be carried out," she demanded with conviction, almost fiercely.

"Why is that?" I asked.

She looked at me imploringly. "Herr Spät. I am allowed to see Papa only once a month. At which time he gives me instructions. His enterprises are complicated, but his overview is amazing. What he tells me to do, I do. He is my father, I am his daughter. You do understand, then, that I obey him."

"Naturally."

Hélène turned fierce. Her anger was real. "Father's private secretary and his lawyers want to put him under the control of a guardian," she confessed. "To my advantage, as they put it. But I know that my father is not mentally ill. And now this commission comes along, the one you've accepted. To Förder it's one more proof. It's pointless, he says. But I am sure that this commission is not pointless."

We fell silent again for a while.

"Even if I don't understand it," she added softly.

"For a lawyer, Fräulein Kohler," I then replied, "the job of investigating the murder of Professor Winter on the assumption that your father was not the murderer has a point, in the legal sense, only if your father is not the murderer. But that assumption is impossible. And thus the commission is pointless. Legally pointless, but it does not therefore have to be scientifically pointless."

She looked at me in astonishment. "How am I to understand that, Herr Spät?" she asked.

"I've been looking around this room, Fräulein Kohler. Your father loves his billiards and his books on natural science..."

"Only those things," she said resolutely.

"Exactly—"

"But that's precisely why he is incapable of committing a murder," she interrupted me. "In some terrible way he must have been forced to do it."

I was silent. I felt that it would have been improper for me to fire off the truth like a cannon. That her father had committed a murder because he loved nothing except his billiards and books on natural science, the abstruse, idiotic truth—I could not have made that clear to her. It was non-sense for me to talk about my vision, it was an intuition, not a fact I could prove.

"I've no information, Fräulein Kohler, about the motive for your father's conviction," I therefore explained cautiously. "I mean something quite different. Something that does not explain what he did, but the job he expects me to do. With this commission, your father wants to explore the realm of the possible. That is his scientific goal, as he himself asserts. I am to keep strictly to that."

"No one can believe that!" Hélène cried out heatedly.

I contradicted her.

"It's up to me to believe it," I declared, "because I've accepted the job. For me it is a game that your father can afford to play. Other people breed racehorses. As a lawyer, I consider your father's game considerably more exciting."

She thought about that.

"I'm sure," she hesitantly replied at last, "that you will find the real murderer, someone who forced Papa to commit murder. I believe in Papa."

Her despair made me feel sorry for her. I would gladly have helped, but I was powerless.

"Fräulein Kohler," I replied, "I want to be honest with you. I don't believe that I'll find that someone. For the simple reason that the someone doesn't exist. Your father doesn't let anyone force him to do anything."

"You're being very honest with me," she said softly.

"I'd like for you to trust me."

She stared into my face, attentive, somber. I didn't avoid her gaze.

"I trust you," she then said.

"I can help you only if you relinquish every hope," I said. "Your father is a murderer. You can comprehend that only if you don't go looking in the wrong place. The motive for your father's crime is to be sought in him, not in someone else. Don't worry any further about this commission of mine. It's my business."

I stood up. She did the same.

"Why have you accepted the job?" Hélène asked.

"Because I need the money, Fräulein Kohler. Don't have any false conceptions about me. Though your father may see some scientific value in his commission, for me it's simply a chance to get my practice moving, but you mustn't let it awaken any false hopes."

"I understand," she said.

"I can't afford to act any differently than I am acting, I have to obey your father's wishes. But you need to know who it is you've put your trust in."

"And I'm sure it's you who will help me," Hélène said and stretched out her hand to me. "I'm happy to have made your acquaintance."

Outside the park, Lienhard was still waiting in his Porsche, but was sitting shotgun now, still smoking cigarettes, absorbed in thought, lost in himself.

"It's all set," I said. "I've accepted the job."

"And the check?" he asked.

"That too."

"Fine," Lienhard said.

I moved in behind the wheel. Lienhard offered me a cigarette, lit it. I smoked, ran both hands over the steering wheel, thought about Hélène and was happy. I was looking forward to the future.

"Well?" Lienhard asked.

I was thinking, had not started the motor yet. "There is only one possibility," I replied. "As far as we're concerned, Kohler is no longer the murderer. We have to play along."

"Agreed."

"Question the witnesses one more time," I continued. "Investigate Winter's past, his acquaintances, his foes."

"Let's get busy with Dr. Benno," he answered.

"With Olympic Heinz?" I asked in amazement.

"Winter's friend," Lienhard declared. "And with Monika Steiermann."

Monika Steiermann was the sole heir to the Trög Amelioratory Works, Ltd.

"Why?" I asked.

"Benno's girlfriend."

"I'd prefer to leave her out of this," I said after some thought.

"Okay," Lienhard replied. Something was not quite kosher.

"Strange," I said.

"What is?" Lienhard asked.

"Kohler recommended you to me."

"Coincidence," Lienhard said.

I started the car and carefully drove off. I had never sat behind the wheel of a Porsche. As we crossed the Train Station

Bridge, Lienhard asked, "Do you know Monika Steiermann, Spät?"

"I've seen her only once."

"Strange," Lienhard said.

I asked him to climb out near Talacker, then drove out of the city. Drove nowhere in particular. Aimlessly out into autumn. The image of Monika Steiermann had shoved its way in front of the image of Hélène Kohler, an image I tried in vain to repress.

II

The Start of the Investigation: My better life commenced with élan. The very next day I had my new office and final possession of the Porsche, though the car turned out to be older than I had assumed and its condition such that the price Lienhard had demanded seemed somewhat less philanthropic. The office had once been that of the former Olympic gold medal winner in fencing and Swiss master in pistol-shooting, Dr. Benno, whose business had been going downhill for some time. Our handsome Olympic Heinz stayed out of the negotiations. He was prepared, as Friedli, the architect, explained to me when he led me over at the crack of dawn, to let me have the office for two thousand a month, with four thousand deposit (I had no idea for whose pocket this sum was meant), but I could move in at once and assume not only Benno's furniture but also his secretary, a somewhat drowsy woman from the Swiss interior with the un-Swiss name of Ilse Freude, who looked like a French barmaid, was forever dyeing her hair a different color, but was amazingly efficient—all in all, a horse trade that was too deep for me. But my new reception room and office on Zeltweg nonetheless befitted my social position, came complete with a view of the obligatory traffic jams, a confidence-inspiring desk, and proper armchairs; facing the courtyard were a kitchen and a room in which I put the couch from my Freiestrasse digs; I couldn't bring myself to part with the old piece. All at once, business seemed to take off. There were prospects for a lucrative divorce case, a trip to Caracas on behalf of a captain of industry beckoned (Kohler had recommended me), inheritance squabbles needed to be settled, a furniture dealer had to be defended in court, plus profitable tax returns. I was in too good and reckless a mood to think about the detective work that I had set in motion, and I would have to wait for a report before I could pursue the Kohler case. Although Lienhard himself should have made me more mistrustful than I already was: The man had something up his sleeve, some murky intentions, had been recommended to me by Kohler, and was all too eager to join up. He was doing a painstaking job of it. He put Schönbächler, one of his best men, to work in the Du Théâtre. The latter owned an old but quite cozy house on Neumarkt. He had had the attic remodeled as a living room and in it had installed his immense stereo system. Loudspeakers were mounted everywhere. Schönbächler loved symphonies. His theory (he was full of theories): Symphonies demanded the least of your attention, you could yawn, eat, read, sleep, converse, etc., to them, their music canceled itself out, became inaudible, like the music of the spheres. He rejected concert halls as barbaric. He made a cult of music. Symphonies were valid only as background music, he maintained, only as a "fond" were they something humane, otherwise it was like being raped; and so only recently, while eating a pot-au-feu, had he understood Beethoven's Ninth for the first time; for Brahms he recommended crossword puzzles, though breaded veal cutlets were good too, for Bruckner, pinochle or poker.

The best thing, however, was to play two symphonies at the same time. Which he did, or so it was said. Well aware of the racket he unleashed, he had worked out a carefully calculated system for the rents paid for each of the other three floors in the house. The apartment under his living room was the cheapest—the renters did not have to pay a cent, just put up with the music, Bruckner for hours on end, Mahler for hours on end, Shostakovich for hours on end; the apartment on the middle floor went for a normal price; the bottom floor was almost prohibitive. Schönbächler was a sensitive man. There was nothing special about his outward appearance; on the contrary, to the outsider he seemed the model citizen personified. He dressed with care, smelled pleasant enough, was never drunk, and lived on the best of terms with the world in general. As regarded his nationality, he called himself a Liechtensteiner. Admittedly, that didn't amount to much, it was his custom to add, but at least he needn't be ashamed of the fact: Liechtenstein bore relatively little guilt for the present state of the world, if one disregarded its printing too many stamps and overlooked its financial improprieties; it was the smallest of countries to live in such a grand style. Nor was a Liechtensteiner easily subject to megalomania, to attributing special worth to himself solely on the basis of his being a Liechtensteiner, as can happen with Americans, Russians, Germans, or the French, who believe a priori that by his very nature a German or a Frenchman is a superior creature. Being a citizen of a great power—and for a Liechtensteiner almost all other countries are necessarily great powers, even Switzerland—carries with it a serious psychological disadvantage: the danger of falling victim to a certain addled sense of proportion. This danger grew, he said, with the size of the nation. He used to elucidate this using the mouse as an example. A mouse, if left all to itself, regards itself as nothing but a mouse, but the moment it finds itself among a million mice, it thinks it's a cat, and among a hundred million mice, an elephant. The most dangerous, however, were the fifty-million-mouse nations (fifty million being the basic unit of his scale). These were made up of mice that thought they were cats but would like to be elephants. These delusions of grandeur were dangerous not only for the mice afflicted with them but at some point for the whole mouse-world as well. The relationship between the "mouse-count" and the resultant megalomania he called Schönbächler's Law. He claimed to be a writer by profession. That may seem astounding, since he had never once written, let alone published, anything. He did not deny it. He simply called himself a potential writer. He was never at a loss for an explanation of why he had written nothing. And so he would occasionally claim that writing begins with its "sense for names," that this was its primary poetic prerequisite, to which you then had to add its no less important moral prerequisite based on the love of truth. When you reflected on these two fundamental prerequisites, it became clear that a title like *Poems by Raoul Schönbächler*, for instance, was out of the question simply because lyric poetry by anyone named Raoul Prettybrook (since that was what his name meant) necessarily awakened visions of poetic babblings and ripplings. Of course someone might object, "Then substitute another name for Schönbächler," but that would put you in conflict with the moral principle based on the love of truth. Wherever Schönbächler turned up, people had something to laugh about. He was a good egg, and a major source of livelihood for many people in the restaurant business. He had everything put on his account and the bills sent him once a month. Added together they must have come to a considerable sum. As regarded his income, this was a matter of some confusion. His claims of a generous stipend from the government of Liechtenstein could not be true, of course. Several people asserted that he was the sales rep for certain rubber articles. Nor could one overlook that he was a man of keen, carefully honed discernment. (Perhaps his not writing wasn't just the laziness it appeared to be, perhaps what lay behind it was the realization that, when you look at the many people who do write, it is better not to write.) He was most famous, however, for his ability to strike up a conversation—particularly since our citizenry is not very good at the art. Whereas Schönbächler was a virtuoso at it. Anecdotes were told, legends arose. There was, for instance, the tale (the commandant swore it was true) that he had once approached a member of the federal cabinet, who was sitting at an adjoining table over four o'clock tea with members of the canton administration, and had got the fellow so entangled in a conversation about our country's relations with Liechtenstein that the cabinet member missed the express train to Bern. It's possible. Though in general one shouldn't give cabinet members all that much credit. On the whole, Schönbächler was considered harmless. No one would have dreamed he was an agent for Lienhard. When that did become known, there was great consternation. Schönbächler left town and now lives with his stereo system in the south of France, much to the distress of our fellow citizens; only recently one of them threatened me with his fist, fortunately I was with Lucky. And so this odd duck, Schönbächler, showed up one day in the Du Théâtre, to everyone's astonishment, since usually he was seen there only rarely. He took a table and stayed the whole day. The next morning he arrived once again, did this for a whole week, chatted with everyone, made friends with the maître d' and the waitresses, but then he disappeared, went back to his old haunts—it had apparently been an intermezzo. In reality, Schönbächler had interrogated the principal witnesses one more time. As far as the rest of the investigation was concerned, however, Lienhard used Feuchting, who was part of the disreputable element that he employed in his detective agency on Talacker, and whom I did not know in those days—I've got to know him only recently (at the Monaco Bar). Feuchting is an undependable, nasty fellow, no one can dispute that, even Lienhard doesn't dispute it, much less the police, who have arrested Feuchting numerous times (heroin) and then turned around and used him for their investigations. Feuchting is a fink, but he knows his job and his underworld. It's possible he once knew better days, that he even went to university—the wretch that's left gets through life by running up bills, by swindling and extorting. It's his rotten luck, or so his commentary (in the Monaco) as he stares gloomily into his glass of Pernod, to have been born a German, not a Russian. You can't make a profession of being German in this neck of the woods, maybe in Egypt or Saudi Arabia, here you can only do it by being Russian. The life he leads wouldn't offend anybody in that case; on the contrary, as a Russian he'd be obligated to live as he does: drunk and broke; but there's no chance whatever that he could do the Russian bit here, because he looks like a German in a French resistance film. On that point he's telling the truth. For once. That is how he looks. He knows both the heights and the depths of society better than anyone else, is a master of the geography of bars and dives. He can find out everything about every regular in the place. But before Lienhard sent me what Schönbächler and Feuchting had dug up, I ran into Monika Steiermann a second time, and what I had feared or hoped—I'm not sure anymore—happened. It would have been better if we had never met (neither the first or second time).

Research in the Public Library: Why not narrate the family history of the Steiermanns? I just received another postcard from Kohler—the last one was four weeks ago, the cat-and-mouse game continues; he says he wants to visit Samoa later, he's going first from Hawaii to Japan—on a luxury liner, while here I was, in front of the board of review and its president, Professor Eugen Leuppinger. The famous criminal attorney, dueling scars on his face, poetic, totally bald, received me in his office; Vice-President Stoss, athletic, ever so manly, modest, merry, and matter-of-fact, was also present. The gentlemen were decent to me. There was no avoiding my being tossed out, the canton senate would request it in any case, and so it would be wiser to steal the march on them, but it was regrettable, one felt the grief a father would, one understood right down the line, sympathized, and was casting no blame whatever, and yet, man to man, hand to your heart, I really did have to admit that, particularly for lawyers, a certain official course of conduct was indicated in a given milieu, that one might indeed put it this way: The more disreputable the one, the more irreproachable the other had to be; the world was, sad to say, a ghastly philistine place, especially our dear hometown, intolerably so, and if only he, Leuppinger, could just slam the door behind him and take off for the south; but that was not the heart of the matter; naturally prostitutes were people too, indeed people of value, poor people, to whom he was personally indebted, he would admit it right here in front of me and his colleague Herr Stoss, for a great many things, warmth, sympathy, understanding, and it went without saying that the law was also there for whores, to use that ominous word, though certainly not in the sense of promoting their trade, and I had to recognize as a lawyer that certain suggestions I had given the demimonde, although incontestable in a juridical sense, had occasioned devastating effects; a knowledge of legal stratagems was catastrophic when placed in the hands of certain circles of society, the police were simply beside themselves, the bar's board of review certainly did not want to dictate here, was not out to terrorize people for their views, was in fact quite liberal, but, well, I knew how it was, statutes were statutes, even unwritten ones; and then, when Stoss had to leave for a moment, Leuppinger asked me, all hail-fellow-well-met, if I couldn't provide him with a certain telephone number so that he could get better acquainted with a certain lady with a fantastic body (Giselle), and then, when he had to leave for a moment, Stoss, all retired jock, asked the same thing. Two weeks later I was disbarred. So here I sit, stone-broke, sometimes at the café that doesn't serve alcohol, sometimes at the Monaco, living more or less on the charity of Lucky and Giselle, with time on my hands, scads of time, which for me is the worst thing possible, and therefore: Why not write up the chronicles of the Steiermann family, which is why I am sitting now in the public library—except, of course, they got quite high-handed when I showed up with a bottle of gin—why not be thorough, painfully scrupulous, why not reveal their background, and anyhow, what are the Steiermanns without the background of their family history and stories? The name is deceptive, the primal Steiermann immigrated, like so many industrialists, from the north, but did so way back in 1191, when a south German duke came up with the wicked notion of founding what is now our federal capital. As is well known, that notion met with success, and so the Steiermanns are prototypical Swiss. As far as the founder of the house is concerned, Jakobus Steiermann, he can be numbered among those scoundrels known to every race and rank; he came to roost in a pirate's nest up on the cliffs above the green river (in those days four hard days' march distant); he was a criminal who, by slipping out of Alsace, had managed to save his head from the Strasbourg executioner; he first got a job as a mercenary in his new hometown but later took up the armorer's trade—a wild, soot-covered fellow. And so down through the centuries the Steiermanns remained tightly bound up with the bloody history of the city; as armorers they manufactured the halberds with which the locals thrashed away at Laupen and St. Jakob, in particular the standard model made by Adrian Steiermann (1212–1255). The family also possessed a chartered license to produce executioner's axes and instruments of torture for all the bishoprics of southern Germany. Their fortunes rose steeply, the blacksmiths on Kesslergasse gained a name and fame. Adrian's son, the bald-headed Berthold Steiermann the

First (Berthold the Black of the saga?), now set to work producing firearms. Even more famous was Berthold's great-grandson, Jakobus the Third (1470–1517). He built such famous guns as the "Four Evangelists," the "Great Psalter," and the "Yellow Urian." The tradition of cannon-making that Jakobus had continued was abruptly halted by his son Berthold the Fourth, who as an Anabaptist forged nothing but plowshares, but it was soon resumed by Berthold's son, who reopened the smithy and began the production of the first grenades as well—though it is true that when the grenades were fired, both he and the cannon were blown to shreds. So much for the truly ancient history. Vivid personalities all, relatively honest, and politically successful—a mayor, two purse-bearers, a high bailiff. In the succeeding centuries, the armor shop gradually became a modern industrial enterprise. The family history gets more complicated, the motifs begin to become covert, the threads are spun out invisibly, the angles and connections aren't just national but international. What was lost in color was gained back in organization, especially in the first half of the nineteenth century, when a latter-day descendant of the primal Steiermann moved to the eastern region of our country. This was Heinrich Steiermann (1799–1877), and he must be regarded as the real founder of the Trög Machine and Armament Works, which came to full bloom under his first grandson, James (1869–1909), and especially under his second grandson, Gabriel (1871–1949). To be sure, no longer as the Trög Machine and Armament Works, but as the Trög Amelioratory Works, Ltd. For in 1891, the twenty-two-year-old James Steiermann became acquainted with the seventy-one-year-old English nurse Florence

Nightingale, under whose influence he transformed the weapon factory into an "Amelioratory Works" for prostheses, which, subsequent to his early death, his brother Gabriel expanded to produce every imaginable kind of prosthesis—hands, arms, legs—and nowadays the Amelioratory Works provides the world with endoprostheses (artificial hips, joints, etc.) and extracorporeal prostheses (artificial kidneys, lungs). "World" is no exaggeration. All this was achieved by stubborn enterprise, by quality control, and above all by the resolute exploitation of market conditions through the ruthless acquisition of all foreign prostheses manufacturers (primarily small operations). This new generation understood the possibilities that the neutrality of our nation offers a manufacturer of prostheses—the freedom, that is, to supply all parties: the victors and the vanquished of the first and second world wars, and nowadays, governmental regulars, partisans, and rebels. Their motto is: "Steiermann for the Victims," even though these days, under Lüdewitz, the production of the Amelioratory Works is again verging more on its original character—the concept of prosthesis is an elastic one. A person will automatically use his hand to try to defend himself against a blow; a shield thus becomes a prosthesis for the hand, or a stone he might throw, a prosthesis for his balled hand, i.e., his fist; once this dialectic is understood, weapons, which the Amelioratory Works has again begun to produce, clearly fall under the concept of prosthesis: tanks, submachine guns, and artillery can be considered a further development of the hand prosthesis. As you can see, a successful clan. And if the Steiermanns were to a man simple, crude, uncomplicated fellows, faithful husbands, often given to drudgery but more often to greed, showing occasionally a refreshing sovereign contempt for the intellect, who got no further at art collecting than one of the weaker versions of the *Island of the Dead*, and who sponsored nothing but soccer when it came to athletics (and that only modestly, as evidenced by the precarious position of the Trög Soccer Club in the A League), the women were of a different caliber. Either great whores or great churchgoers, though never both together, whereby the whores were always ugly, with heavy cheekbones, long noses, and wide, tight-lipped mouths, whereas the pious ones were women of exquisite beauty. As far as Monika Steiermann goes, who unexpectedly was to play a major role, indeed a double role, in the Dr.h.c. Isaak Kohler affair, judging by her looks she belonged to the churchgoers, by her lifestyle, to the great whores. After the death of her parents (Gabriel Steiermann married Stefanie Lüdewitz in 1920), who were killed in a plane crash on a flight to London (or more precisely: were lost, since neither parents nor their private plane was ever found), and after the tragic end of her brother, Fritz, who went diving off the Côte d'Azur and never resurfaced, she (born in 1930) inherited the handsomest fortune in our country, and the prostheses firm was directed by her maternal uncle. Monika's lifestyle was, to be sure, more difficult to direct. The wildest and often most ridiculous rumors about this girl circulated, hardened then into almost-certainties, dissolved again, were denied—always by Uncle Lüdewitz—and for precisely that reason were believed anew, until they were surpassed by other, even grander, scandals, outdoing all the rest, and the sport began all over again. People gazed with disapproval on this amoral heiress of countless millions, but with secret pride as well, with envy (she can have anything she wants), yet with gratitude—they were getting something for their money. La Steiermann was the official "world-ranked femme fatale" of a city whose reputation on the one hand was kept afloat by the desperate, strenuous efforts of local authorities, churches, and community organizations, only to be called into question on the other by its hustlers—it was they, and our banks, not our hookers, who gave our city international renown. People breathed what was almost a sigh of relief. Our twofold reputation for being simultaneously both prudish and queer was placed on a correction course toward more commonplace vices by La Steiermann. The young lady grew ever more popular, especially after our mayor began weaving her into the notorious extemporaneous speeches and hexameters to which he frequently treats us after official ceremonies have dragged on for hours, when some literary prize is being awarded, for instance, or on the occasion of the anniversary of some private bank or other. But there was a very definite reason why I feared meeting Monika Steiermann a second time. I had come to know her through Mock. Back in my Stüssi-Leupin days. His studio near Schaffhauserplatz was overheated in the winter, the cast-iron stove glowed red, the air was downright toxic from pipes, cigars, and cigarettes, everything incredibly filthy besides, with wet towels eternally draped around unfinished torsos, between them piles of books, newspapers, unopened letters, wine bottles, whiskey bottles, sketches, photographs, shaved smoked beef. I had come to see the statue that Mock had made of La Steiermann, was curious because he had told me he was going to paint the statue. The sculpture stood in the middle of the overwhelming disorder of the studio, frighteningly realistic, life-size and true in every detail. Made of plaster of Paris, painted flesh color, as Mock explained. Stark naked and in an unambiguously ambiguous pose. I gazed at the statue for a long time, amazed that Mock could do this too. He was usually a master of intimation: he worked free-style, with a few blows heaving what he wanted out of his stones, which often weighed in at several hundred pounds. An eye emerged, a mouth, a breast maybe, a vagina, he didn't need to hew the rest, from such hints the fantasy of the observer would create the head of a Cyclops perhaps, or some beast, or a female. Even when he made molds, he made do with the barest essentials. You must mold just as you sketch, he would say. All the more astonishing, then, was his procedure here. The plaster seemed to breathe, and above all was painted to perfection. I stepped back and then moved in close again; to make the illusion more perfect, he must have used human hair for the head and pubic area. And yet the statue had nothing doll-like about it. It radiated a remarkable plasticity. Suddenly it moved. It got down off the pedestal, not deigning me a glance, walked to the back of the studio, looked for, found, a half-full bottle of whiskey and drank. She was not made of plaster of Paris. Mock had lied. It was the genuine Monika Steiermann.

"You're the fourth person to fall for it," Mock said, "and you made the dumbest face. And you don't know anything about art either."

I left. The statue of painted plaster, which was standing in another corner of the studio, was picked up the next day. By an agent of Freiherr von Lüdewitz, the uncle who managed the Trög Amelioratory Works, Ltd.

*

Monika Steiermann I: The further I get with this report, the harder it becomes to tell the story. Not only is the report getting confused, my role is also becoming equivocal. I am no longer able to state whether I was dealing on my own, or if others were dealing through me, or if in fact I was the deal. Above all, my doubts are growing whether it was pure chance the way Lienhard brought Monika Steiermann into it. I had had no luck with my furniture dealer. He had in fact had a fictive expert from Rome declare genuine a Renaissance armoire that had been made on Gagerneck and had then affixed the fictional signature to it—something that escaped my notice, but not Jämmerlin's. But the trip to Caracas still lay before me, and in the midst of the preparations Ilse Freude announced a certain Fanter, another one of Lienhard's men. To my amazement in walked Fanter, a fat man smoking a Brissago, wearing the uniform of a policeman, having served his city in that capacity for two decades.

"You're crazy, Fanter, to appear in public like that."

"It'll be useful, Herr Spät," he sighed, "it'll be useful. Monika Steiermann called. She needs a lawyer."

"Why?" I asked.

"She's getting beat up."

"By whom?"

"Dr. Benno," Fanter replied.

"And why?"

"She caught him in bed with another woman."

"Then she should beat him up. Funny, isn't it? And why should I be the one to worry about La Steiermann's problems?"

"Lienhard is no lawyer," Fanter answered.

"Where is she?"

"Why, with Dr. Benno."

"Damn it, Fanter, don't beat around the bush, where's Benno?"

"You're the one beating around the bush with your questions," Fanter declared. "Benno is beating up Monika Steiermann at the Breitingerhof. The Prince von Cuxhafen is there too."

"The auto racer?"

"That's the one."

I called the Breitingerhof and asked for Dr. Benno. The manager, Pedroli, came to the phone. Who was calling?

"Spät, I'm a lawyer."

"He's beating up Steiermann again," Pedroli laughed. "Go to your window, you can hear it."

"I'm over on Zeltweg."

"Doesn't matter. Echoes all over the city," Pedroli declared. "The guests are fleeing my five-star hotel."

I had parked my Porsche on Sprecherstrasse. Fanter got in next to me, and off we drove.

"Use Hegibachstrasse," Fanter said.

"The long way around," I objected.

"Not to worry. La Steiermann can take a lot."

At a stop sign near Klusstrasse, Fanter got out.

"Drive by here on your way back," he said.

End of October. The trees red and yellow. Leaves in the streets. As I pulled up, Monika Steiermann was already waiting in front of the Breitingerhof, wearing nothing but a man's black pajamas, its left sleeve missing. Tall. Red-haired.

Cynical. Beautiful. Freezing. Her left eye was blackened and swollen shut. Had been struck across the mouth. Her naked arm badly scratched. She waved at me, spitting blood in a wide arc. Benno was raging at the hotel entrance, he, too, bruised and scratched, held back by two bellhops, the hotel windows full of people. Curious, grinning onlookers surrounded Steiermann, a policeman was directing traffic. In a white sports car sat a glum young blond man, Cuxhafen, presumably, a young Siegfried, obviously ready to pull away. Pedroli, the small and agile manager, came out of the hotel and laid a fur coat over Steiermann's shoulders, an expensive one I'm sure, I don't know anything about furs. "You're freezing, Monika, you're freezing."

"I hate fur coats, you asshole," she said and flung the fur over his head.

I stopped next to her. "Lienhard sent me," I said. "Spät, I'm a lawyer. Spät."

She climbed painfully into the Porsche.

"Beat to a pulp," I observed.

She nodded. Then she stared at me. I was just about to drive off, but her gaze disconcerted me.

"Haven't we met somewhere before?" she asked, speaking with difficulty.

"No," I lied and pulled away.

"Cuxhafen is following us," she said.

"So what."

"He's a race driver."

"Formula one."

"We won't be able to shake him."

"The hell we won't. Where to?"

"To Lienhard's," she said, "to his house."

"Does Cuxhafen know where Lienhard lives?" I asked.

"He doesn't even know Lienhard exists."

At the stop sign at Hegibachstrasse I pulled obediently to a halt. Fanter was standing on the sidewalk in his police uniform, walked over to the Porsche, demanded my license. I gave it to him, he checked it, nodded politely. Then he turned to Cuxhafen, who had had to pull up behind me, and started carefully checking his ID. Then he walked all around his car, slowly, fussily, constantly checking the papers. In the rearview mirror I noticed Cuxhafen cursing. I saw as well how he had to get out, how Fanter dug out a notebook, and then I drove down Klusstrasse toward the lake, down Höhenweg, onto Biberlinstrasse and then to Adlisberg, just for safety's sake made several detours, then raced up Katzenschwanzstrasse to Lienhard's bungalow.

I parked beside the front gate. The chalet next door had to be Jämmerlin's. I had read that he was turning sixty today, which explained all the cars on a street that would normally be empty. He was having a garden party. Stüssi-Leupin was just driving up. Monika Steiermann followed me in her black pajamas up the steep stairs, cursing. Stüssi-Leupin had got out of his car and was looking over at us, apparently amused. Jämmerlin's disapproving face popped up over the hedge.

"Here," Steiermann said and handed me a key. I opened the front door, let Steiermann in ahead of me. The front door led immediately into the living space. A modern room with antique furniture. Through an open door you could see into a bedroom with a comfortable bed. She sat down on a divan, looking up at a Picasso above an antique chest. "He painted me."

"I know," I said.

She regarded me, amused. "And now I remember where I know you from," she said. "From Mock's. I played a statue for you."

"It's possible," I replied.

"You were terribly frightened," she recalled. Then she asked, "Didn't you like what you saw that day, is that why you've forgotten me?"

"Oh, sure I did, sure," I admitted. "I liked it a lot."

"So then you haven't forgotten me."

"Not entirely," I admitted.

She laughed. "Well then, since you remember." She stood up and took off the pajamas, stood there stark naked, brazen and exciting, indifferent—that was more than apparent—to the dreadful thrashing Benno had given her. She walked up to the large window, from which you could see across to Jämmerlin's. The guests assembled there stared our way, Jämmerlin with binoculars, beside him Stüssi-Leupin, who waved. Monika assumed the pose of the statue that Mock had made of her, Stüssi-Leupin applauded, Jämmerlin raised a menacing fist.

"Many thanks for rescuing me," Steiermann said, still holding her pose so her audience could view her, her back toward me.

"A coincidence," I replied. "Lienhard asked me to do it."

"I'm always getting beaten up," she said wistfully. "First by Benno and then by Cuxhafen. And the others have always beaten me up too." She turned toward me again.

"Well, that's a basis for rapprochement," I said. "Your right eye's swelling shut too."

"So what?"

"Should I scare up a wet compress?" I asked.

"Bull," she said, "but you'll find cognac and glasses in the cupboard."

I opened an old Engadine cupboard and found what she asked for, poured it.

"You've been here often, I take it?" I asked.

"A few times. I guess I'm a real whore," she declared, with some bitterness and some bewilderment, and yet grandly.

I laughed. "They get treated better."

She emptied her glass of cognac and then said, "Now I'm going to have a hot bath."

She limped into the bedroom. Vanished. I heard water running, curses. Then she came back, demanded another cognac.

I poured it. "Are you sure that's good for you, Monika?"

"Nonsense," she replied. "I've got the constitution of a horse." Then she limped away again.

When I entered the bathroom, she was lying in the tub and soaping up. "Burns like hell," she said.

I sat down on the rim of the tub. Her face darkened.

"Do you know what I'm going to do?" she asked, and when I didn't, answered, "I'm going to hang it up. Hang it up."

I didn't respond.

"I am not Monika Steiermann," she explained nonchalantly. I stared at her in astonishment.

"I am not Monika Steiermann," she repeated, and then said calmly: "I'm only leading the life of Monika Steiermann. My father was Professor Winter."

Silence. I didn't know what to think of this.

"And your mother?" I asked and knew as soon as I had that it was a stupid question. What did I care about her mother.

It made no difference to her. "A teacher," she answered, "in the Emme Valley. Winter dumped her. He was always dumping teachers."

She noted this without animosity.

"My name's Daphne. Daphne Müller." Then she laughed. "Nobody ought to have a name like that."

"If you're not Monika Steiermann, then who is Monika Steiermann?" I asked in confusion. "Does she even exist?"

"Ask Lüdewitz," she replied.

Then she pulled up short. "Is this an interrogation?" she asked.

"You asked for a lawyer. I'm a lawyer."

"I'll let you know when I need you," she suddenly replied, thinking hard, turning almost hostile.

Lienhard appeared. I hadn't heard him come in. He was simply there all of a sudden. He tamped down one of his Dunhills. "Satisfied, Spät?" he asked.

"I don't know," I answered.

"Satisfied, Daphne?" he asked.

"So so," she answered.

"I brought you some clothes," he said.

"I've got Benno's pajamas," she asserted.

Outside an ambulance was howling our way.

"Jämmerlin must have had another heart attack," said Lienhard dryly. "I gave him sixty roses."

"And he saw me naked." She laughed.

"That's nothing new for you," he suggested.

"How do you know who Daphne is, Lienhard?" I asked.

"You just stumble on that sort of thing. Sometimes," he answered and set fire to his Dunhill. "Where can I take you from here, Fräulein Müller?"

“To Ascona.”

“I’ll drive you.”

“Good businessman,” she declared approvingly.

“Goes on the expense account,” Lienhard said. “He pays that.” He pointed at me. “He’s gained some priceless information.”

“I have another job for him,” Daphne said.

“Well?” Lienhard asked.

Her right eye, not swollen quite shut yet, sparkled, and she passed her left hand through her cinnabar red hair.

“He’s to inform the genuine Monika Steiermann, that lesbian nanny goat, that I don’t want to see her again. If she gets it from a lawyer, it’s official.”

Lienhard laughed. “Girl, there’s going to be scandal you can’t even imagine.”

“What do I care,” she said.

Lienhard’s Dunhill just wouldn’t burn right in the steamy bathroom. He relit it.

“Spät,” he suggested, “don’t get mixed up in this. That’s my advice.”

“You’ve already got me mixed up in it,” I answered.

“That’s true too,” Lienhard said and laughed, and then to Daphne he said, “Climb out.”

“You’ve turned into a real orator,” I declared to Lienhard and left.

Later, on Zeltweg, I gave Lüdewitz a call. He ranted. I knew too much. He was chagrined. And that’s how my visit to the real Monika Steiermann came about.

Second Address to the Prosecutor: The more I write, the more improbable my report becomes. I putter away mightily at being literary, even attempt a poetic tone, record the weather conditions, attempt to be geographically accurate, check my city map, all of it just because you, Herr Prosecutor Joachim Feuser (please forgive the dead man in the morgue for speaking to you personally again), are fond of things literary, things poetic, and in general regard yourself as man of the muses, as you love to mention on every possible and impossible occasion, even before juries, and thus, without my literary trimmings, just might fling my manuscript into some corner. But my report remains a cliché. Despite the poesy. So sorry. I feel like the author of a trashy novel: me the fanatic for justice, Lienhard the Sherlock Holmes on the River Limmat, and Daphne Müller the Messalina of the Gold Coast, as the right bank of our lake is called. The statue with the sturdy breasts and the indecent pose, which I overlooked at Mock's while admiring the living Daphne as a statue, that sensuous female made of painted plaster of Paris (not to mention the genuine one) has with the passage of time become more lively in my memory than the girl who appears in my report. Of course it's immaterial whether, and if so, how often, she slept with Lienhard—who didn't she sleep with?—but people's inner motives and processes are after all essential to my report—how things come about in this convoluted world and why. If the external event is correct, the interior motive can be guessed at, even if it can't be nailed down with certainty; if the external facts are incorrect, if intercourse occurred and it is not registered, or if one mentions it when it did not occur, one hovers in a vacuum, in the void. As is the case here. How did Lienhard discover the secret of the "false" Monika Steiermann? By sleeping with her? Then a great many people would have known it. Did she love him? Then she wouldn't have told him. Was she afraid? Possibly. And as far as Benno goes, was Lienhard bent on suspecting him from the beginning? Was Daphne the reason? I ask these questions because people have laid the blame for Daphne's death at my door—I shouldn't have gone to see the genuine Monika Steiermann. But Daphne had asked me to. I had to pursue a possible lead. I had accepted the job and the advance of fifteen thousand francs, even though I believed in the impossibility of the possibility—and still believe in it, for there is no doubt that Dr.h.c. Isaak Kohler murdered Winter. That it could have been someone else is only a possibility, but one that means nothing; the fiction that I had to posit for my search, the fiction that Kohler was not the murderer, necessarily implied the possibility of neglected facts coming to light. For the rest, I have to write the truth, stick to the truth, and yet: What is the truth behind the truth? I stand before guesswork, grope about. What is correct? What is exaggeration? What's been tampered with? What's been hushed up? Which things should I doubt? Which believe? Is there anything true, certain, definite, behind these events, behind these Kohlers, Steiermanns, Stüssi-Leupins, Lienhards, Hélènes, Bennos, etc., who have crossed my path, anything true, certain, definite, real, behind this city of ours, behind this country of ours? Isn't all this irredeemably encapsulated, hopelessly excluded from the laws and motives that keep the rest of the world moving and breathing, isn't this just a provincial Central European backwater, isn't all this unreal—all that lives, loves, guzzles, swindles, scrambles and fusses here, goes on breeding and organizing? What do we still represent? What do we still stand for? Is there one kernel of sense, one grain of meaning in the whole kit and caboodle I'm describing? But perhaps the answer to the question lies lurking behind it all, perhaps it will unexpectedly break out of each conceivable human situation and constellation, like an assault from an ambush. The answer will be the judgment spoken upon us, and the carrying out of that judgment, the truth. I want to believe that. Passionately and steadfastly. Not for the sake of the exquisite society in which I vegetate, not for the sake of these intolerable relics that surround me, but for the sake of justice, for the love of which I act, must act, in the hope of preserving my last scrap of humanity (what I am writing here is of solemn, lofty, holy pathos and high seriousness with organ accompaniment, but I won't cross it out, won't make corrections, and why should I, why make any attempt at style—I am guided not by literary ambitions but by homicidal intent, and by the way: not drunk, Herr Prosecutor, you err, not drunk, but sober, stone-cold sober, fatally sober). Therefore I have no other choice (to your health, Herr Prosecutor!) but to drink, to whore, to report, to register my doubts, to punctuate with question marks, and to wait, to wait, until truth reveals itself, until that cruel goddess unveils herself (getting literary after all, makes me want to vomit). That will not happen on these pages, the truth is not a formula that can be jotted down, it lies outside every attempt at speech, outside all poesy, only when justice bursts upon us, only when justice carries out its own eternal execution of justice, will it take effect, only then will we surmise it. Truth will be when one day I stand before Dr.h.c. Kohler, eye to eye, when I effect justice and execute its judgment. Then there will come a moment, a beat of the heart, a lightning bolt of eternity, one long second lashing out in a shot, when truth flashes forth, the truth that's melting away now as I think about it, that seems hardly more than a bizarre and evil fairy tale. Just as my visit to the "genuine" Steiermann seems to have been: more dream than reality, more legend than fact.

Monika Steiermann II: Mon Repos is on the edge of our city, set in such a gigantic and overgrown park that the villa has long since become almost invisible; only in winter can you painstakingly surmise, over toward Wagnerbühl, a few indistinct walls and a gable through the tangled branches of old trees. Very few people can still recall social gatherings at Mon Repos. Even the "genuine" Monika's father and grandfather had given their parties and celebrated their anniversaries at country homes on Lake Zug and Lake Geneva, spending time in our city only to work (they were the personification of industrialist drudgery), they did their celebrating elsewhere, and the ladies, if they did visit our city, resided at the Dolder, at the Baur au Lac, or indeed at the Breitingerhof. Mon Repos became more and more a legend, especially after one morning when three burglars, who had traveled here from Germany, were found lying beaten to a pulp at the gate leading to the park of the Steiermann villa; the police had no comment. Lüdewitz had intervened. Except for Daphne, whom people regarded as Monika Steiermann, no one appeared to spend any time in the house, deliveries had to be left in an empty garage beside the gate to the park, and yet the grocery orders were sizable. Daphne herself never invited anyone to the villa; she had an additional apartment on Aurorastrasse. I had taken a couple of painkillers while driving to Wagnerstutzweg. The upended weather had upended yet again; the lake looked like a ditch, so near was the far shore. Four in the afternoon. I stopped at the entrance to the park. The gate was unlocked. I walked into the park, unsure of myself, the pills were still working. The gravel path led uphill, with a wooden step now and then, but it was not at all as steep as I had expected—*Stutz*, after all, means a steep incline. The park was uncared-for, the paths hadn't been weeded, the fountains were overgrown with moss, junglelike patches were scattered here and there, and all of it populated by scads of plaster gnomes. They were placed not as separate individuals but in groups, in clans—brainless, with white beards, pink, smiling, idiotic, some were even sitting in the trees, fastened there like birds on the branches; then came still larger gnomes, grimmer, more malicious, and female ones too, bigger than the males, eerie gnome women with large heads. I felt followed, encircled, walked faster and faster until, coming out of a sharp curve around a mighty old ash tree, I was abruptly intercepted. It was as if I had slammed up against iron, but I was unable to get a good look at the person I was bouncing up against. I was turned around, apparently by a bodyguard, who more carried than walked me the rest of the way to the villa. At the front door stood a second bodyguard, a fellow so massive he seemed to fill the door frame, who took me over and shoved me inside, first through a vestibule, then through a hall with a crackling fireplace—what looked like a whole tree trunk was burning in it—and finally into a drawing room, or, if you will, a den. I was dropped into a leather armchair. I looked up, dazed. My arms and back hurt. Both bodyguards were sitting across from me in bulky leather armchairs. They were bald. Their faces were like clay. Slant-eyed, cheekbones like fists. They were impeccably dressed, dark blue suits of pure silk, as if this were the middle of summer, white silk ties, but with shoes like the ones weight lifters wear. Though they weren't especially tall, the effect was of two colossuses. I nodded to them. Their faces remained expressionless. I looked about me. The wainscoted walls were hung and pasted full of photographs, so many that the dark brown paneling was almost papered over with them; and with the strange kind of fright that accompanies such a discovery, I realized that the same person was pictured over and over again: Dr. Benno; and only then did I spot, against the barred window of a niche in the opposite wall, Mock's salacious masterpiece of sculpture, the naked "false" Steiermann, Daphne, but now in bronze, with both hands lifting her breasts like weights. Just as I noticed it, the double door across from it opened and a third bald-headed bodyguard—even more massive, even more silken than the two in their leather armchairs—entered carrying a wrinkled and misshapen creature the size of a four-year-old child. Draping the tiny crippled body was a grotesque black dress with a plunging neckline, and a sparkling sapphire.

"I am Monika Steiermann," the creature said.

I stood up. "I'm Spät, the lawyer."

"I see, I see, a lawyer," the tiny creature with the ponderous head replied. The weirdest thing was the voice. It was as if another person's voice were coming from this freak. It was the voice of a woman. "What do you want of me?"

The bodyguard, with the creature in his arms, stood there immobile.

"Monika—"

"Frau Steiermann," the creature corrected me, and then

tugged at its dress. "Dior. Chic, don't you think?" In its voice was cool, haughty mockery.

"Frau Steiermann, Daphne does not want to return here to you ever again."

"And you're to inform me of that?" the creature asked.

"I was asked to inform you," I answered.

There was no guessing how the creature took the message.

"Whiskey?" it asked.

"Love some."

Without the creature's giving any signal, the double door behind me opened and a fourth bald-headed bodyguard brought in scotch and ice.

"Straight?" it asked.

"On the rocks."

The fourth bodyguard served me, stayed on. The first two had stood up now too.

"How do you like my servants, Mr. Lawyer?" the creature asked, and the one carrying it put the scotch to its mouth.

"Impressive," I said. "I thought they were your bodyguards."

"Impressive, but stupid," it replied. "Uzbeks. The Russians got hold of them somewhere in deepest Asia and stuck them in the Red Army, then they ended up prisoners of the Germans, and since the Nazi anthropologists couldn't agree on what race they were, they managed to stay alive. My father bought them at an institute for race research. You could get beasts like these very cheap in those days. Mankind's useless left-over inventory. I call them Uzbeks because I like the word. Have you seen our garden gnomes, Mr. Lawyer?"

The sweat was streaming down my face. The room was overheated.

"A whole army of them, Frau Steiermann."

"Sometimes I have them put me among the females," the creature said, laughing, "and nobody notices me, even when I move. Cheers."

The Uzbek carrying it held the scotch to its lips again. It drank.

"To your health, Frau Steiermann," I said and took a drink myself.

"Sit down, Lawyer Spät," it commanded. I sat down in the leather armchair. The immobile Uzbek stood in front of me, the creature in his arm.

"So Daphne doesn't want to return to me," it said. "I always knew that someday she wouldn't come back," and in its little creased face tears appeared in the big eyes beneath the massive, almost hairless skull.

Before I could say anything, the Uzbek placed the creature on my lap, pressed its glass of scotch in my free hand and, facing the window, fell to his knees, together with the other three. Their rear ends flew up. The creature clutched at me. I felt rather clumsy holding the two glasses.

"They're praying again. Five times a day. Usually they set me down on a cupboard," it said.

Then the creature commanded: "Drink."

I held the glass to its lips.

"Isn't Olympic Heinz simply beautiful?" it asked out of the blue and only then chugged its scotch.

"Certainly is," I replied and put the empty glass on the carpet beside my leather armchair. As I did, the creature almost fell off my lap.

"Nonsense," it said in a dark voice full of self-contempt.

"Benno is a degenerate, cheap lady-killer that I've fallen in love with. I'm always falling in love with cheap men, because Daphne is always falling in love with cheap men."

The creature I was holding in my arms felt like a tiny skeleton.

"I gave Daphne my name so that she could live the life I would have liked to live, and she's lived it," it declared. "I would have slept with everybody too. Have you slept with her too?" the creature asked, the voice dry and cool all of a sudden.

"No, Frau Steiermann."

"Cut the prayers!" it commanded.

The Uzbeks stood up. The one who had carried the creature in his arms took it back. I had automatically stood up as well, my whiskey on the rocks still in my hand. I had carried out my task and wanted to take my leave.

"Sit back down, Mr. Lawyer," it commanded. I obeyed. From the arms of the Uzbek it looked down at me. There was something menacing in its eyes now. Banned inside the little, crippled body, it could only express itself through its eyes and its voice.

"A knife," it said.

One of the Uzbeks flipped open a switchblade, handed it to the creature.

"To the Benno pictures," it said.

The Uzbek carried it to the photographs on the walls, and, as if operating on him, it calmly shredded the smiling Dr. Benno, shredded Dr. Benno as he meditated, slept, beamed, drank, shredded Dr. Benno in his tails, in his dinner jacket, in his tailored suit, in his riding breeches, shredded Dr. Benno as he shot his pistol, played the pirate at a costume ball, in his swimming trunks, without his swimming trunks, shredded Dr. Benno in his fencing garb at the Olympics, shredded Dr. Benno in his tennis outfit, Dr. Benno in his pajamas, Dr. Benno out hunting—we made room for her. I was surrounded by Uzbeks, the one carrying the little creature circled about us in the infernal heat of the den while scraps of shredded photographs began to cover the floor. When all had been shredded, we resumed our seats as if nothing had happened. The creature was again placed on my lap. I sat there like a father with an aborted monstrosity.

"That did me good," it said calmly. "Now I'll dump Daphne. I'll see to it that she becomes what she once was."

It looked up at me. The creased face seemed very ancient, as if the creature had been born before there were human beings.

"Give my regards to old Kohler," it said. "He used to visit me often. Whenever I would get angry because he wanted to have his own way, I'd climb around in the library and throw books at him. But he always got his way. He's still managing my affairs. From prison. That we've gone into the production of armored tanks and antiaircraft guns, mortars and howitzers, instead of optics and electronics, is Kohler's doing. Do you think Lüdewitz is capable of that, or me? Just look at me."

The creature fell silent.

"I've got nothing but bats in my belfry," it then said, and the scorn and contempt in which the misshapen creature held itself was once again apparent.

"Carry me out," it commanded.

The Uzbek picked it up in its arm.

"Adieu, Mr. Lawyer Spät," it said, cool, haughty mockery once again in its voice. The French doors were opened and the Uzbek bore Monika Steiermann out. The French doors closed again. I was alone with the two that had brought me in. They walked over to my leather armchair. One of them took the glass of whiskey from my hand—I was about to get up, but the other one pushed me back down. Then he threw the scotch in my face. The ice had melted. The two grabbed me up out of my chair, carried me out of the den, through the hall, out the front door, down through the park, past the garden gnomes, opened the entrance gate and tossed me in front of my Porsche. An old married couple walking along the sidewalk stared in amazement, first at me and then at the Uzbeks, who were soon lost from sight in the park.

"Guest workers," I said and pocketed the ticket the police had wedged under the windshield wiper. Blocking driveways is illegal.

Report on a Summary Report of Reports: Three days after my visit to Wagnerstutz, the communiqué appeared in our world-famous local paper. It was written by a certain Äschisburger, member of Parliament and attorney for the Trög Amelioratory Works, Ltd.: The person who, once she had been turned loose from a boarding school on the Côte d'Azur, had kept our city holding its breath with her scandals for ten years now was not Monika Steiermann. She had been passing herself off as such with the kind permission of the physically handicapped heiress of the Trög Amelioratory Works, Ltd., but in reality she had been born Daphne Müller on 9 September 1930, the illegitimate child of Ernestine Müller, a teacher in Schangnau, canton of Bern, and of Adolf Winter, lecturer at our local university, who was murdered on 25 March 1955. This press announcement, recorded here in much the same manner as the MP handed it out, awakened the scandal that Äschisburger had intended it should; the press, always courteous until now, became ruthless, even the thrashing at the Breitingerhof was described in detail, with Pedroli disclosing that Benno owed him for three months' room and board and that whereas he had assumed that Monika Steiermann would pay in the end, it had turned out that La Steiermann wasn't La Steiermann at all. Neither Daphne nor Benno could be located; the mob came howling down on me, Äschisburger having hinted that I had visited the genuine Steiermann; Ilse Freude fought back like a lioness, several reporters shoved their way into my office all the same, I saved my hide with vague generalities, imprudently naming Cuxhafen, whom Pedroli hadn't mentioned, and the mob was off and running to Reims: too late, Cuxhafen's new Maserati had exploded during a trial heat, scattering both its own and the prince's parts; on return to our city, the reporters besieged Mon Repos, caravans of cars on Wagnerstutz, no one was allowed into the park, let alone the villa; one reckless fellow who climbed over the wall at night equipped with all sorts of hi-tech apparatus found himself the next morning, with no idea how it had happened, outside the entrance gate, sans clothes and cameras, lying naked in the slush, for overnight and simultaneous with the communiqué, autumn had fallen upon our city, a storm wind had swept the trees of their rusty brown and yellow hues, then rain had set in, then snow, then rain, filthy sloppy mush covered the city, and there the reporter stood in it, freezing. But the scandal not only set the presses rolling, it enkindled imaginations. The town hatched the most asinine rumors, to which I paid no attention for much too long. I was too busy with my own problems. My clients began to drop away, the trip to Caracas fell through, the lucrative divorce fizzled out, no one at the tax office would trust me. My new start, begun with such hope, suddenly looked hopeless, Kohler's advance was gone, I felt I had started to run a marathon as if it were the hundred meters and now there lay ahead an endless stretch before my law practice could begin turning a profit. Ilse Freude started looking for a new job. I confronted her.

She was sitting in the reception room behind her desk, had placed a small mirror on her keyboard and was painting her lips carmine. Her hair, which yesterday had been blond as straw, was black with a hint of blue that looked more like green. It was five minutes before six.

"You've been spying on me, Herr Spät!" Ilse Freude protested and went on putting on her makeup.

"Well, when you talk that loud on the phone with the employment agency," I defended myself.

"I presume I'm allowed to sound things out," she replied, having finished with her makeup, "but I won't leave you high and dry, what with this mountain of work that's ahead of us."

"What mountain of work?" I asked in astonishment.

Ilse Freude did not answer at first, but set her all-but-bursting shoulder bag on the desk and carelessly tossed in her mirror and lipstick.

"Herr Spät," she declared, "you look harmless enough, much too kindhearted for a lawyer, lawyers aren't supposed to look like that. I know lawyers, and their looks either inspire confidence or there's something artsy about them, like pianists, but without the tails, but you, Herr Spät—"

"What's your point?" I interrupted impatiently.

"My point is that you're a sly dog, Herr Spät. You don't look like a lawyer, but you are one. And you want to free that innocent canton deputy from prison, too."

"What is all this nonsense, Ilse?" I said in amazement.

"Why else would you have received a check for fifteen thousand francs from Deputy Kohler?"

I was dumbfounded. "How do you know about that?" I snapped at her.

"I do have to straighten up your desk every once in a while," she spat back, "what with the mess you leave. And now you're bullying me."

She wiped her eyes. "But we'll manage. You just get that nice canton deputy out. I'll stick with you. Like a burr! We'll manage it together, Herr Spät!"

"You believe old man Kohler is innocent?" I asked, aghast.

Ilse Freude stood up gracefully, despite her respectable fullness, hung her bag over her shoulder.

"Why, the whole town knows that," she said. "And who the real murderer is, too."

"Well now I'm all ears," I said and a sudden chill ran over me.

"Dr. Benno," Ilse declared. "He was Swiss master in pistol shooting. It's in all the newspapers."

Later I had dinner with Mock at the Du Théâtre. He had invited me, a rarity for that old tightwad. I accepted the invitation, although I knew that Mock invited people only when he was sure they would decline. But I was curious to know whether it was true that ever since Winter's murder Mock had been dining at his table. It was true. To my surprise, Mock greeted me amiably, but hardly had I taken my seat when the commandant joined us—the first time I had ever met him—and it turned out that he had come in order to make my acquaintance, had in fact organized our get-together, was our host and paid for everything at the end as well. Mock had only been the bait. The commandant ordered liver-dumpling soup, tournedos rossini with home fries and green beans, plus a bottle of Chambertin, in memory of Winter, as he put it, who had been a dreadful gasbag, it was true, but a splendid chowhound. It had always been a joy to watch him go at it. I had the same. Mock chose from the cart: roast beef with mashed potatoes. There was something macabre about the meal. We ate in silence, so it was really quite unnecessary for Mock to lay his hearing aid next to his plate so that he could eat in peace. Then the commandant ordered a mousse au chocolat, and I told him about my conversation with Ilse Freude.

"You've no idea, Spät, just how right your oddball secretary is. The rumor started at the prison. The warden and the guards all swear that Kohler cannot possibly be the murderer. How that old crook has managed it, hell only knows. But let a few people believe some bit of nonsense and others will believe it as well. It's like an avalanche. Larger and larger chunks of believers in nonsense come tumbling down. At first it was the homicide squad itself that believed it. Well, you see, it's really no concern of yours, Spät, but Lieutenant Herren is not well liked, and his squad would be more than happy if it turned out that Kohler's arrest was a mistake, and as for the rest of the police force, they're jealous of the homicide squad, while the fire department and the employees of the traffic division suffer from an inferiority complex over against the police, and now the avalanche can't be stopped and has reached the general population, who rejoice in our every setback anyway. In mine especially, and all at once the murderer has been turned into an innocent lamb. And then you add the fact that it was a popular murder, one that suited a lot of people to begin with, and that the guilds and the circle around Kohler—the senators, the members of Parliament, the cabinet, the canton deputies, the town council and whoever else has their finger in the pie, all the general directors, the bosses and execs—are annoyed by the energetic way Jämmerlin proceeded and the way the judges fell right over for him. They have nothing against a guilty verdict, but they had counted on a sentence with probation or even on an acquittal on grounds of temporary insanity, which of course doesn't count as insanity in a politician. Kohler's innocence would be a balm for many wounds, Spät."

Mock shoved his plate away and plugged his hearing aid into his ear.

"Kohler has given you a very strange commission, and now there's all this idiotic talk that he's innocent and that windbag Benno is the murderer. Just because he's a crack shot, in a country where everyone imagines himself one. But why did the numbskull have to go into hiding?" the commandant said and went to work on his mousse au chocolat. "Don't like it. Kohler's commission, the rumor that he's innocent, and Benno's disappearance all fit together somehow."

"Spät has fallen into a trap," Mock said and began to draw on the tablecloth with a charcoal crayon: a rat, caught in the trap, but still gnawing at the bacon.

Back on Zeltweg, Lienhard was sitting in my office.

"How did you get in?" I asked indignantly.

"That's unimportant," Lienhard replied and pointed at my desk. "The reports."

"Do you think Kohler is innocent too?" I asked, my suspicions aroused.

"No."

"Mock thinks I've fallen into a trap," I said gloomily.

"Depends on you," Lienhard answered.

A hundred fifty pages, typed single-spaced, telegram style. Where I had expected a hypothetical discussion, vague conjectures, here I stood with facts in my hand. Instead of persons unknown, there was a name. The reports themselves were of varying worth, and were generally to be greeted with caution. The interrogation of witnesses by Schönbächler: Witnesses do contradict one another, but the extent of contradiction here was amazing. Examples: One waitress maintained that Kohler had shouted "Bastard," while the manager of a lingerie shop who was sitting at the next table that day ("I got splashed with gravy"), stated that Kohler's words had been "Good day, old friend." A third witness claimed to have seen the canton deputy shake hands with the professor. One of them said that after he had shot Winter dead, Kohler had run smack into Lienhard. A question mark was appended here, with Lienhard's notation: "Wasn't there." Further contradictory testimony covering more than fifty pages. Now there is no such thing as an objective witness. Every witness tends to blend subconscious invention into his experience. An event to which he is witness takes place both outside and inside the witness. He perceives the event in his own way, imprints the event on his memory, and his memory goes on reimprinting. His memory reproduces a very different event. And then the discrepancies were multiplied because Schönbächler, in contrast to the police, had interrogated *all* the witnesses. The more witnesses, the more contradictory the statements; the contradictions filled over fifty pages. Finally, there was the passage of time: The event had occurred a year and nine months before. Fantasy had had time to reshape memory, and then there was wishful thinking, grandstanding, etc.—another fifty pages could have been filled with the statements of those people who imagined they were present at the murder but weren't. But Schönbächler had made a careful investigation. Feuchting's report: His methods were the simplest. He asked direct questions—he could afford to, because he always asked direct questions. It didn't even attract attention when he made inquiries. He made inquiries about everything, even about things that were nonsensical, or that appeared to be nonsensical. At the end, he pieced his stones together, ever so painfully, with the glue of countless martinis, to form a mosaic that was thought-provoking, since it confirmed the statements of the various witnesses appearing in Schönbächler's report, several of whom claimed that Dr. Benno had also been at the Du Théâtre; others, that he had approached the professor before Kohler had; and still others, that he had sat at the same table; and one who even stated that he had left the restaurant immediately after the canton deputy; and a bar waitress testified that shortly after Winter's murder, Benno had burst into the bar, dancing with joy, breaking glasses, and shouting, "The louse is dead, the louse is dead," elbowing everyone and declaring that he would marry her now. People had assumed he meant Steiermann, had congratulated him and had accepted invitations to the wedding. All of this had taken place at the Sky-High Bar, so named because of its potent schnapps, a thieves' den near the cathedral where Benno had often been seen of late. In Benno's case this "of late" had been going on now for more than two years. He came from a good home, had had a good education and top honors in school, a career in sports, brilliant success in society, an engagement to Steiermann, the wealthiest match in the city—but Benno had suddenly deteriorated, had changed, was shunned. It was generally assumed that Steiermann had broken off the engagement. A lot of foreign trips, rumors that he was gambling. At first he was still able with some effort to maintain his connections with good, lucrative families, but soon was no longer on their invitation lists, and was finally boycotted. He was still living in grand style but had turned to selling off whatever he could rescue from his former days of glory: etchings, furniture, several crates of vintage Bordeaux. A few items he sold had not belonged to him, pieces of jewelry and such, two lawsuits were pending. (I shall pass over an exact accounting of Olympic Heinz's debts, they were catastrophic, absolutely bizarre, more than twenty million all told.) Strangely enough, Feuchting's findings about Benno were equally valid for Winter, the murder victim (except for the debts): foreign trips to PEN Club conventions that had never been held but about which he would talk for weeks, rumors about visits to casinos. Winter, too, had been hanging around the Sky-High Bar, bringing with him his penchant for quoting Goethe—once he had left the third floor of the Du Théâtre and the table frequented by the literati. There he would sit with the publishers, editors, theater critics and the litero-hagiographic authorities of our city, part of their joint effort to prevent control of our city's culture from slipping out of their hands. That illustrious circle tolerated him, but with mocking smiles, and called him Mahadöh when he would run off to his Niederdorf go-go girls. It was doubtless true, Lienhard said in conclusion, that if one excluded Kohler as the murderer, Benno was the only other possible perpetrator. He had believed Daphne was Monika Steiermann. Then something had happened between him and Winter. As a result of that incident, Daphne had broken things off with Benno, and Benno had gone bankrupt. As Steiermann's fiancé his credit was unlimited; without Steiermann he had none. I felt my mistrust growing. Lienhard's version did not fit the facts. Daphne had ended her affair with Benno only after he had beaten her, and Monika Steiermann had dropped Benno only after Daphne had called things off with her. Winter and Lüdewitz had known that Daphne was not Monika Steiermann, but they weren't the only ones. For someone to assume another person's identity and vanish into thin air herself is not an easy matter; other parties have to be in on the secret. A few people in the government bureaucracy must have known. And Kohler had known too. Steiermann herself had told me that. Maybe a great many people had known. The trap into which, according to Mock, I had fallen could only consist of my having willy-nilly fueled the fires of belief in Kohler's innocence, even when I did not share that belief. I had been made a part of it by taking on Kohler's commission. In yielding to the fiction that he was not the murderer, I had to run smack into another murderer—if it wasn't Brutus who slew

Caesar, then it was Cassius; it if wasn't Cassius it was Casca. Maybe. Maybe it wasn't the warden and the guards who had started the rumor that Kohler was innocent, maybe it was me. How did the commandant know about my commission? The guard, Möser, had been present when he gave it to me; the Knulpes, Hélène, Förder, Kohler's private secretary, plus various lawyers, and Lienhard, and then which of his men? Ilse Freude knew—could she keep her mouth shut? Maybe Kohler's commission was already the talk of the town; I was of course convinced that he had committed the murder out of scientific curiosity, but by taking on the job I had let my research lead away from Kohler instead of to him. Had that been the point of his commission? By delivering the investigative reports to the man who commissioned them, would I be the prime mover of some obscure maneuver? But I was in a bind. Lienhard would soon present his expense account. I needed money, and my only source of money was Kohler. I had to go on. Despite my scruples. Or was there a way out? It occurred to me to track down my erstwhile boss, Stüssi-Leupin, and consult with him. But I hesitated. Then I decided that I wouldn't go to him after all, nor deliver the reports, come what might. And then I hesitated no longer. Dr. Benno paid me a visit in the night between Friday, November 30, and Saturday, December 2, 1956. Around midnight. I don't remember precisely. Because on that night his fate was decided—and my own. I was sitting at what had been his desk, studying the report for the third time, when he flung open the door to the office that had once belonged to him. He was a big man, turned ponderous, with long stringy black hair combed across to cover his bald head. He limped over to my desk. The effect was of a man who had grown too heavy for the framework of his bones. He propped himself against the desk top with hands that, in comparison with his ponderous body, seemed almost childlike, stared at me from the half-light of the desk lamp. He was no longer sober, a desperate man whose helplessness awakened sympathy. I leaned back. His black suit was shiny and greasy.

"Dr. Benno," I said, "where have you been? The reporters have been looking for you everywhere."

"Makes no difference where I've been," he gasped. "Spät, leave this trial alone. I beg you."

"What trial, Dr. Benno?" I asked.

"The one you're trying to drag me into," he said in a hoarse voice.

I shook my head. "No one is trying to bring you to trial, Dr. Benno," I explained.

"You're lying," he shouted. "You're lying! You've set Lienhard on me, Fanter, Schönbächler, Feuchting. And you've got the press at my heels too. You know that I could have had a motive for shooting Winter."

"Kohler shot him," I replied.

"You don't believe that yourself." His whole body was trembling.

"No one doubts it," I said, trying to mollify him.

Benno stared at me, wiped his brow with a dirty handkerchief. "You're trying to bring me to trial," he said softly. "I'm ruined, I know it, I'm ruined."

"Really now, Dr. Benno," I replied.

He staggered to the door, opened it slowly and left without bothering any further with me.

*

The Alibi: Was interrupted again. Fate struck. This time through Lucky. Accompanying him, a personage whom he introduced as "the Marquis." (To the extent that I am now stepping out of the disastrous tale I am writing about, a tale in which I am involved as a participant, I must show my colors: In a criminal world I have become a criminal myself. I am confident that you will agree with that observation, Herr Prosecutor, though of course with the qualification that I also count you, and the society you officially represent, as part of that criminal world, and not just Lucky, the Marquis, and myself.) As far as this personage with some resemblance to a human being goes, he had been flushed this way from Neuchâtel. Along with a Jaguar convertible. A visage with a smile, as if the fellow belonged to the moral majority at Caux, with the manners of a salesman for expensive soaps. It was close to ten o'clock at night. It was a Sunday (I'm writing this report at the end of July 1958, a weak attempt at setting my papers in order). There was a thunderstorm going on outside, incredible booming explosions, the rain still roaring, but without having brought any relief, it was sultry and oppressive. Beneath me psalms were rumbling: "Sink, O world, in Jesus' arms, perish now rejoicing" and "Holy Ghost, with bolts and claps, lead us sinners to collapse." Lucky was tugging somewhat embarrassedly at his moustache, seemed a little nervous to me, and his apostolic eyes even had an introspective shimmer about them that I had never noticed before: Lucky was apparently mulling things over. They both had on raincoats, though they were practically dry.

"We need an alibi," Lucky said dejectedly, "the Marquis and I. For the last two hours."

The Marquis smiled unctuously.

"And two hours ago?" I asked.

"We've got a watertight alibi," Lucky assured me with a sly look. "We were with Giselle and Madeleine at the Monaco."

The Marquis nodded in agreement.

I wanted to know if they had got in here without anyone seeing them. Lucky was as always an optimist. "Nobody recognized us," he declared. "Umbrellas are useful."

I considered this. "Where are your umbrellas?" I then asked, getting up from my desk and locking up my papers.

"Downstairs. We left them behind the door to the cellar."

"Do they belong to you?"

"We found them."

"Where?"

"At the Monaco."

"So you're saying you pilfered them two hours ago?"

"It was raining."

Lucky was worried, he sensed I wasn't exactly enthusiastic about his answers. But full of hope, he pulled a bottle of Napoléon cognac from his coat, and the Marquis conjured up a second one and put it on the desk.

"Fine," I nodded, "I call that a humane gesture."

Then each of them put down a thousand-franc bill.

"We're top-notch businessmen," Lucky observed.

I shook my head. "My dear Lucky," I said with regret, "it's one of my principles not to do time for perjury."

"Got it," Lucky said.

They came up with another thousand apiece.

I wasn't about to be softened up. "This business with the umbrellas is just too stupid for me," I remarked.

"The police aren't looking for us on account of those umbrellas," Lucky objected, although he was obviously uneasy about it.

"But they could pick up your trail on account of those umbrellas," I reminded him.

"Got it," Lucky said.

They sacrificed another thousand each.

I marveled. "Have you both turned into millionaires?"

"A fellow has his sources of income," Lucky said. "When we get hold of the rest, we're beating it. Getting out of the country."

"What rest?"

"The rest of our fee," the Marquis declared.

"What fee?" I asked with suspicion.

"For a job we did," Lucky said, getting down to details. "Once we're in Nice, I'll pass Giselle and Madeleine on to you."

"I'll pass my girls on to you too," the Marquis assured me. "Neuchâtel is a good market."

I carefully examined the bills, folded them and stuck them in my back pants pocket. Lucky wanted to provide details, but I interrupted him. "For once and for all: I don't want to know why you need this alibi."

"Sorry," Lucky apologized.

"Fork over your cigarettes," I demanded.

Lucky was stuffed full with cigarettes: Camel, Dunhill, Black and White, Super King, Piccadilly. The packs were heaped up on the desk.

"A girlfriend runs a kiosk," he apologized.

"And what does the Herr Marquis smoke?"

"I seldom smoke," he lisped in embarrassment.

"You haven't got any cigarettes on you?"

The Marquis shook his head.

I sat back down behind the desk. We had to act. "Now we're going to smoke for a half hour," I decreed, "as much and as fast as we can. I'll take the Camels, Lucky the Super Kings, and the Marquis the Dunhills for chrissake. Smoke the cigarettes down to where the brand can still be seen, then put them out, and all in the same ashtray. When we're done we'll each take the open pack with us."

We puffed away as if our lives depended on it. We soon figured out to light four cigarettes at once, then let them burn down on their own. Outside the thunderstorm started rumbling away again, and the psalms came howling up from downstairs: "Crush, O Lord, our adder's nest, shatter, Christ, our wealth ill-gained; Thee we slaughtered, of hopes the best, the Holy Ghost we have disdained."

"I normally don't smoke at all," the Marquis groaned. He was feeling so queasy he seemed almost human.

A half hour later, the cigarette butts built a mound in the ashtray. The air was toxic, since we had kept the window closed. We left the room and ran down one flight of stairs, right into the arms of the police, but their visit was intended not for us but for the Saints of Uetli. Neighbors, desiring to go to hell unaccompanied by psalms, had complained. Fat old Stuber from the vice squad rattled the door, his two companions, cops from the beat, eyed us mistrustfully, we were well-known characters.

"My good Stuber," I said, "you're with the vice squad and saints are no concern of yours."

"Just you take care of your own saints," Stuber growled and let us pass.

"Shyster, hooker-shyster," one of the cops from the beat called after me.

"The best thing would be to march right down to the precinct," Lucky moaned. The police had demoralized him. The Marquis seemed to be praying for sheer terror. I had a hunch I had got myself into some ticklish business.

"Nonsense." I bucked them both up. "Best thing that could have happened, having the police run into us."

"The umbrellas…"

"I'll get rid of them later."

The fresh air did us good. The rain had stopped. The streets were busy, and when we got to Niederdorfstrasse we went into the Monaco. Giselle was still there, Madeleine was gone (I know her name now), but in her place were Corinne and Paulette, the new girls in Lucky's employ, just imported from Geneva, all three of them dolled up in their best, to match their prices, and with several tricks already behind them.

"The Marquis looks green around the gills," Giselle cried out and waved. "What did you do to him?"

"We played poker for two hours," I explained, "and made the Marquis smoke along with us. As punishment for thinking he could take you away from Lucky."

"Je m'en suis pas rendue compte," Paulette said.

"Deals are best done on the sly."

"Et le résultat?"

"I'm your lawyer now," I explained. That took Paulette by surprise. I turned to Alphons, the bartender. He had a harelip and was washing glasses behind the counter. I asked for whiskey. Alphons set three Sixty-nines in front of us. I chugged mine, told the bartender, "These gentlemen are paying," and left the Monaco. I was barely ten steps from the door when I heard a car stop. I saw the commandant enter the bar with three detectives from the homicide squad. I slipped around the nearest corner and into the next bar. And I had a piece of good luck later too (for once at least): Stuber and the two cops were no longer in the house on Spiegelgasse when I returned an hour later. It was quiet, even the Uetli brethren must have made themselves scarce. I found both umbrellas behind the cellar door. I was just about to descend into the cellar to hide them there when I got another idea. I climbed the stairs. It was quiet at the door to the sect's premises. It wasn't locked; if it had been I would have opened it with the house key, which, as is often the case with old houses, fit all the doors.

I entered a vestibule. The only dim light came from the stairwell. Next to the door was an umbrella stand with several umbrellas. I put both damp umbrellas with the others, carefully closed the door, and climbed on up to my apartment. I turned on the light. The window was wide open. The commandant was sitting in the armchair.

"Somebody did a lot of smoking in here," he said and glanced at the ashtray full of butts. "I opened the window."

"Lucky and the Marquis were here," I explained.

"The Marquis?"

"Some guy from Neuchâtel."

"What's his name?"

"I prefer not to know."

"Henry Zuppey," the commandant said. "When were they here with you?"

"From seven to nine."

"Had it rained yet when they arrived?" the commandant asked.

"They arrived before the rain started," I answered. "To keep from getting soaked. Why?"

The commandant regarded the ashtray. "Stuber from vice saw you, Lucky and the Marquis leaving your digs at nine. Where did you go from here?"

"Me?"

"You."

"To the Höck. I had two whiskeys. Lucky and the Marquis went to the Monaco."

"I know," the commandant said. "I just arrested them there. But now I'm going to have to let them go. They have an alibi. They were here smoking with you. For two hours." He regarded the ashtray again. "I have to believe you, Spät. A man who cares so much about justice doesn't provide two murderers with an alibi. That would be absurd."

"Who's been murdered?" I asked.

"Daphne," the commandant replied. "The girl who pretended she was Monika Steiermann."

I sat down behind my desk.

"I know you know all about that," the commandant said. "You paid a visit to the genuine Monika Steiermann, who then dumped the false one, and so Daphne Müller ended up working the streets. Without having made arrangements with Lucky and Zuppey. And now they found her dead in her Mercedes in a parking lot on Hirschenplatz. Around eight-thirty. She arrived at seven, but stayed in her car. It was raining cats and dogs. Well, Lucky and Zuppey have an alibi now and they didn't have a weapon on them, and their raincoats were dry. I'll have to let them go." He fell silent. "A damned beautiful woman," he then said. "Did you sleep with her?"

I didn't answer.

"It's of no importance," the commandant remarked and lit one of his Bahianos, coughed.

"You smoke too much, Commandant."

"I know, Spät," the commandant answered. "We all smoke too much." He looked at the ashtray again. "But I notice you have a certain amount of concern for me. Well, now I'm going to show a certain amount of concern for you: I've never come across such an enigmatic person as you. Do you have any friends at all?"

"I'm not much interested in making enemies," I replied. "Is this an interrogation, Commandant?"

"Just curious, Spät," the commandant sidestepped. "You're not even thirty yet."

"I couldn't afford to dawdle my way through university," I replied.

"You were our youngest lawyer ever," the commandant remarked, "and now you aren't a lawyer anymore."

"The review board did its duty," I said.

"If only I could get some image of you in my mind," the commandant said, "it'd be easier for me to figure you out. But I can't find the image. The first time I paid you a visit, your struggle for justice seemed plausible, and I felt a little shabby, but you're not plausible at all now. I'll accept this alibi of yours, but that you care about justice—that I no longer accept."

The commandant stood up. "I feel sorry for you, Spät. You've got yourself involved in an absurd affair, that much is clear, and it's caused you to become absurd yourself—but that probably can't be changed. I assume that's why you've let yourself sink to this. Has Kohler written you again?"

"From Jamaica," I answered.

"How long has he been gone now?"

"Over a year," I said, "almost a year and a half."

"The fellow's whizzing back and forth around the globe," the commandant said. "But maybe he'll return soon."

Then he left.

Postscript: Three days later now. That I had slept with Daphne was something I concealed from the commandant. He didn't pursue it really, nor was it important to him. I have thought long about whether I ought to record the fact here. But the commandant is right, it's all become so pointless that there's no point in concealing anything. Even the most shameful things are part of reality, and my role in Daphne's downfall was a shameful one, even if the real reason was an act of revenge by the "genuine" Monika Steiermann. After the scandal broke, Daphne was nowhere to be found for almost a year. No one knew where she was, not even Lienhard, or so he claimed. Her apartment on Aurorastrasse remained empty, but the rent was paid. By whom, no one knew. Then she reappeared. In all her old glory. As if nothing had happened, though with a new retinue. What she had formerly done out of extravagance she now did professionally. Having been left in the lurch by her friends, she now made the rounds in her white Mercedes, demanded a horrendous price, and got herself back on her financial feet. Despite taxes. Local taxes, national taxes, army taxes, old age insurance, widows' and orphans' insurance. It was considered chic to sleep with her; there's no need to wax epic. But neither do I want to conceal the fact that she did show up once at my place. About two in the morning she knocked at the door to my apartment on Spiegelgasse. I crept from the couch that I used as a bed, thinking it must be Lucky, turned on the light, opened the door, and in she walked. She looked around her. The window was half open, the room ice-cold (it was the middle of February), the "aerial views" were back up on the walls, my clothes were on the desk, my coat over the armchair. She was wearing a chinchilla—the story about her high price must have been true, or else the "genuine" Steiermann was still paying—she took off her clothes, tossing everything over the armchair, and lay down on my couch. I lay down beside her. She was beautiful, and it was cold. She didn't stay long. She dressed again, reached for her chinchilla and laid a thousand-franc bill on my desk. When I protested, she slapped me in the face with her right hand, as hard as she could. One doesn't enjoy telling a story like that, and I have never told it to anyone. And though I'm putting it down here, it's only because every hope has been washed downriver. This morning, shortly before six, our friend Stuber from vice was here and reported that they had fished Lucky and the Marquis out of the lake (Steiermann's villa is not far from where they were found). I was somewhat hurt when cheerful Stuber left again: He hadn't asked me a single question; the commandant could at least have sent someone from the homicide squad. Lucky and the Marquis hadn't made tracks out of the country fast enough. And so our national holiday, the First of August, 1958, began rather dismally. Besides which it was a Friday, besides which

Daphne was being buried—the coroner had released the body for burial. At ten o'clock. On the First of August, people work until noon, even the gravediggers, a whole national holiday is too much for a small nation, we're aware of our dimensions. I had just left my room when it began to thunder, thunderstorms being pretty much an everyday occurrence this summer. My VW is at the shop. (I had been parked above some lake or other, and then as the night turned wild and stormy, my Porsche and I—ah yes, Herr Prosecutor, this too I confess—and Madeleine [was it Madeleine?] skidded off Tüfweg into the bushes; Lucky took care of the whole thing, the girl was in the hospital for two months, and I had my old VW back. Had. I had had it back. I could have picked it up long ago, but my credit has run out with the garage. I am afraid of my bills.) So I had to take a streetcar to Daphne's funeral. Why it was exactly that I pushed down on the handle of the door to the Assembly Hall of the Saints of Uetli and why, when the door opened, I grabbed one of the two umbrellas that I had left there six days before, is no longer clear to me. Was it out of pure thoughtlessness or some macabre sense of humor? I don't know anymore. Although it was only nine-thirty, the sky had already turned dark black as I ran through the old city to the Bellevue, using my umbrella like a walking stick. The whole world seemed nervous, and I was in a hurry, the way you are before a thunderstorm, and the one that was about to break must be a beauty, since it was still morning. Typical Daphne, I thought. From the Bellevue I took the streetcar. Actually, given the weather conditions, it was nonsense to go to a funeral, but I climbed mechanically into the overfilled streetcar all the same. Now and again the sun broke through the black wall of clouds, as if a spotlight were being turned on and off. At Kreuzplatz, a stout but rather small man got on—he was clad in black, had a shiny bald head, well-kempt black beard streaked with white, and gold rimless glasses. The fellow looked so much like Winter that I automatically thought at first it must be the murdered man returned as ghost to attend the burial of his daughter, and he was carrying a funeral wreath, though I couldn't read the inscription on the ribbons. A great many people were already gathered at the cemetery. All the local celebrities were present, no one is immune from nostalgia; none of her new clients had showed up. But Daphne Müller was not the only reason to pay a visit to our trimly planted municipal cemetery that morning. In the grave next to hers, Prosecutor Jämmerlin was being entrusted to eternity. His demise was likewise a matter of general sorrow, since there is indeed nothing sadder than no longer having something to be annoyed at. Fortunately, the mourning was well mixed with schadenfreude. His end had not lacked for comedy. He was at the sauna, which he visited once a week, had sat down naked next to the naked Lienhard, and had proved quite incapable of surviving the shock. And so people mourned up their sleeves. The simultaneous burials had their advantage, too. You could take part in both at the same time. I pondered who had come to whose burial—the mayor, Prosecutor Feuser, and several acquitted sodomites to Jämmerlin's, in hopes of harassing the dead man in his grave; Lienhard, Leuppinger, Stoss, and Stüssi-Leupin to both; while Friedli, Lüdewitz, and Mondschein were probably there for Daphne's interment. Everyone had brought an umbrella along. Pastor Senn stood beside Daphne's grave,

Pastor Wattenwyl beside Jämmerlin's. Both ready to go. I waited impatiently, shifting my weight from one leg to the other. It thundered. But neither Pastor Senn nor Pastor Wattenwyl began to pray. The elderly man I had met in the streetcar had set down his wreath (there were no others beside the coffin), TO MY HALF-SISTER DAPHNE, HUGO WINTER. This had to be Winter the grammar school teacher. It thundered again, this time a mighty crack. A gust of wind. Everyone waited and waited, the people at the neighboring grave even looked over our way, they were all waiting for something. I didn't know for what, until I noticed: From the entrance to the cemetery came a wheelchair, the "genuine" Monika Steiermann was being shoved in march rhythm toward the coffin by a gaunt nurse. The dwarf had made herself up garishly, a cinnabar wig sat atop her head, in imitation of Daphne's hair, making the little woman's head larger still; she was wearing a miniskirt, which looked like a baby's frock, and a pearl necklace that hung down over the wheelchair, dangling between her crippled legs; in her lap she held an object wrapped in black cloth. Next to her walked a thickset man in a dark suit that was too short and tight for him, the filthy-rich boor Äschisburger, MP. He was dragging a wreath behind him. Even the mayor and Feuser, in fact the gravediggers as well, left Jämmerlin's grave and moved over to Daphne Müller's. Pastor Wattenwyl stood alone. He probably would have loved to join them. Renewed cracks of thunder, more gusts of wind.

"Damn," someone beside me said. It was the commandant.

The nurse had pushed Steiermann up to the open grave, Äschisburger tossed his wreath on the coffin, the ribbon read TO MY BELOVED MONIKA, YOUR MONIKA.

Pastor Senn stepped forward, flinched at the next crack of thunder, and all in attendance moved in closer. Against my will, I was pressed up right behind Steiermann and found myself between the nurse and the commandant; in front of him was Äschisburger, and in front of the nurse, Stüssi-Leupin. The coffin was lowered into the grave. There was no one at the adjoining grave to lower Jämmerlin's coffin, Pastor Wattenwyl was still gazing over our way, Pastor Senn timorously opened his Bible, announced John, chapter 8, verses 5 to 11, but never got to read his text. Monika Steiermann lifted up the object she had been carrying and smashed it, with a strength no one would have thought her capable of, into the grave, thumping it down onto Daphne's coffin with such force that it broke through the lid. It was the bronze head of Mock's "false" Monika Steiermann. Pastor Wattenwyl came stumbling over, and Pastor Senn was so terrified and confused that he automatically said: "Let us pray."

But here came the first heavy raindrops, the gusts kneaded themselves into a storm wind, and the umbrellas opened up. Since I was standing behind Steiermann, I wanted to protect the dwarf and opened my own as well. I pressed a button down near the handle, and to my bewilderment my bumpershoot flew off, ascended, circled above the gathered mourners, and fell, as the wind suddenly died, into Daphne's grave like a great black bird. A lot of people had to suppress their laughter. I stared at the umbrella handle I was holding in my hand: It was a stiletto. I realized I might well be standing guard at the grave of the murdered woman with the murder weapon in my hand, while the pastor said the Lord's Prayer. Then the gravediggers began to work away with their shovels, and the coffin with Jämmerlin inside could be lowered now as well. The nurse rolled Steiermann away, I had to make way for her but was still standing there with my stiletto, umbrellas closing all around: The thunderstorm, sparing our cemetery out of piety, was unleashing itself on the center of town—cellars were still being pumped out late that evening—while lightning flashed all about. People were celebrating now. Garish, overpowering sunlight flooded the shoveling gravediggers and the thronging crowd as it exited the cemetery. Pastor Senn saw to it that he got out of there as quickly as possible, and Pastor Wattenwyl just hung around in total confusion; the mayor and Feuser had already left. Only Lienhard was still standing at Jämmerlin's grave, watching it being shoveled full. As he walked by me he was weeping. He had lost an enemy. I stared down at the stiletto again. Its tip was dark brown, as was the groove in the thin blade.

"Your umbrella is no longer useable, Spät," the commandant, standing next to me, remarked; he took the umbrella-handled stiletto out of my hand and started off for the cemetery exit.

The Sale: A postcard Kohler sent from Hiroshima has reassured me, he's going on to Singapore. Finally have time to report the crucial material, even if it was as stupid as it is crucial, and as inexcusable, despite my financial straits. I sent Stüssi-Leupin the reports, and two days later he received me in the living room of his home some distance from the city. The term living room is an understatement—more like an uninhabited hall. The room is square, I'd guess sixty feet by sixty feet, three sides of it glass, no door visible anywhere;

beyond one of the walls is a view down to an old town, through which, since it has been spared an autobahn, an endless line of cars rolls, lending the landscape a lively, ghostly look in the dusk as chains of light move along the arteries of the old walls; through the other two glass walls you look up to erratic blocks, lighted from the rear, tons and tons of mass that Mock has hewn into those granite gods that ruled the earth before man, ripping mountains up out of the depths, rending continents apart, monoliths, casting gigantic phallic shadows into the empty hall—for except for a grand piano, the only other furnishings were two club chairs placed on a diagonal across from it. The grand piano stood almost at the entrance, in the worst conceivable spot, next to a wooden stairway that led to a gallery, which must have led to several rather small rooms, since the house had looked to me, as I drove up in my Porsche, to be all on one floor, and I recalled that from the town below I had thought it was a bungalow. In one of the two club chairs sat my former boss, wrapped in a bathrobe, immobile, illumined only by a floor lamp between the two chairs. I cleared my throat, he didn't move, I walked across the multicolored ingeniously patterned marble tiles that covered the hall floor, Stüssi-Leupin still didn't move. I sat down in the other club chair, sinking into a sea of leather. Beside the chair I discovered an uncorked bottle of red wine sitting in a basket on the floor, a small tulip-shaped crystal glass, and a bowl of nuts; the same items were placed beside the club chair in which Stüssi-Leupin sat, about twelve feet away, except that there was also a telephone in front of him on the floor. I gazed at Stüssi-Leupin. He was sleeping. I thought of the portrait Varlin had done of him, which I had always considered exaggerated, for only now did I realize the genius with which the artist had captured him: under a tangled pelt of snow-white hair, a square peasant skull, brutally hewn into shape, a nose like some sort of tuber, deep creases that led down to the chiseled chin, the unspeakably defiant and yet gentle mouth. I looked at this face as if it were a familiar and yet puzzling landscape, for I knew little about Stüssi-Leupin; although he had been my boss for several years, he had never exchanged a single personal word with me, which was perhaps the reason I didn't stay with his firm.

I waited. All at once his astonished childlike eyes were staring at me through his rimless glasses.

"Why aren't you drinking, Spät?" he said, wide awake, as if he hadn't been sleeping at all (and maybe he hadn't been). "Pour yourself some wine, I'm going to do the same for myself."

We drank. He watched me, said not a word and watched me.

Before we got around to speaking about this difficulty, he began, gazing straight ahead, and though he could well imagine the basis of that difficulty, he would like to add a personal comment, one that likewise had to do with the scruples now plaguing me, which had sent me marching off to him—well, well, that wasn't quite right either, I had driven up in a Porsche after all, posh, posh.

He laughed to himself—something seemed to amuse him immensely—took a drink and continued. Had he ever told me his own life story. No? But why should he have. Fine. He was the son of a farmer up in the mountains, and his family was called Stüssi-Leupin to avoid confusion with the Stüssi-Bierlins, with whom they had, from time out of mind, been feuding over a potato field that was so steep they had to cart it back up into place every year, often several times a year, a field that with good luck yielded enough potatoes for three, four, servings of home fries, and yet on account of which people sued, thrashed and murdered one another. Were still at it. To be brief, after finishing his studies, he had moved back to his home village as a lawyer, to the Stüssi village, as it was called, and not only were the Stüssi-Leupins at daggers with the Stüssi-Bierlins, but also the Stüssi-Moosi with the Stüssi-Sütterlins, and so on through the whole Stüssi clan, though that had been the case only at the very beginning, at the founding of the village, if there had ever been such a thing, nowadays every Stüssi family was on the outs with every other one. And in that mountain podunk, Spät, in that rat's nest of family intrigue, murder, incest, perjury, theft, embezzlement, and libel, he had spent his apprenticeship as a lawyer for farmers, as their spokesman, as they called attorneys there, not with the intention of bringing justice to the valley, but to keep it out: A farmer who arranged an accident for his old lady and then married his dairymaid, or a farmer's wife who, after she had deftly applied some arsenic to send the old man to the cemetery, married the farmhand—they were of more use on their farms than in prison. Empty prisons cost the state less than full ones, or vacant farms, and so the webs were woven and the beloved soil slid into the valley.

He laughed to himself.

"God, what a time that was!" he marveled. "And then the devil must have put a burr up my ass, and I go and marry a von Melchior, move to the lousy city, and become a star lawyer. What's the weather like?"

"The foehn is blowing. Much too warm for December," I replied. "Like spring."

"Shall we go outside?"

"Fine with me," I answered.

"'Go' is perhaps not quite the right word," he declared, pressed a button on the arm of his club chair, and the oversized glass walls sank into the floor, the floodlights behind the erratics went out. We sat beneath the floating concrete ceiling as if under the open sky, illuminated only by the floor lamp.

A swanky piece of architecture, he declared, staring straight ahead. He felt like the Führer in his Reichskanzlei. But what else could you expect, Spät, as a star lawyer he had had to put up a Van der Heussen, although he would have preferred a podunk Friedli. Fate—you get to be all the rage. At one time these walls saw one party after another, the people in the little town had complained, podunkers all, until—well, that wasn't the point. He had had the furniture removed. All modern stuff.

Then, pouring himself more wine, he said, "Let's get to the point, Spät."

I told him about Dr.h.c. Isaak Kohler's commission.

He knew all about that, Stüssi-Leupin interrupted my explanation, drank, the Knulpes had visited him as well. Hélène, Kohler's daughter, had informed him about my commission, and he had studied Lienhard & Co.'s investigative reports.

I told him about my thoughts as to Kohler's motive, about Hélène's suspicion that he had been forced to commit murder, reported as well my meeting with Daphne, my visit to see the genuine Monika Steiermann, and how Benno had popped up at my office.

"Young man, what an opportunity," Stüssi-Leupin said with amazement and again poured himself some wine.

"I don't understand what you mean," I replied uncertainly.

"But of course you understand," Stüssi-Leupin countered. "Otherwise you wouldn't have come to me. Let's assume we go along with Kohler's game. Once we assume he is not the murderer, then another murderer is damned easy to find. It can only be Benno, which is why he's wobbling at the knees. He went through over twenty million francs of the woman he presumed was Steiermann; Winter lets the genuine Steiermann know, the engagement falls apart, Benno is ruined, guns Winter down in the Du Théâtre. Voilà. That's the version your employer needs and that you're going to need as well."

Stüssi-Leupin held his glass up to the light of the floor lamp. Honking horns could be heard coming from the little town below, kept up for several minutes—to judge by the motionless headlights, the lines of traffic had clogged.

Stüssi-Leupin laughed. "And the loveliest appeal case of the century falls into the lap of a greenhorn like you, of all people."

"I have no commission to take over an appeal," I said.

"The commission you have taken over leads directly to it."

"Kohler murdered Winter," I declared.

Stüssi-Leupin showed his amazement. "So what?" he said. "Were you there?"

At the back of the room a dark figure came down the stairs and limped toward us. As it moved nearer, I realized that it was a priest carrying a small black handbag. He stopped about ten feet away from Stüssi-Leupin, coughed, the panes of glass rose back up, the floodlights came back on, the granite gods cast their shadows into the reencased room. The priest was ancient, lopsided, wrinkled, and had a clubfoot.

"Your wife has received the last rites," he said.

"Okay," Stüssi-Leupin said.

"I shall say prayers," the priest assured him.

"For whom?" Stüssi-Leupin asked.

"For your wife," the priest specified.

"That's your job," Stüssi-Leupin replied listlessly, nor did he look up as the priest muttered something and limped toward the exit, where the housekeeper, who had let me in, opened the door for him.

"My wife is dying," Stüssi-Leupin remarked offhandedly and finished off his glass of wine.

"In that case…" I stammered and got up.

"My God, Spät, you are squeamish," Stüssi-Leupin said. "Sit down!"

I sat down, he poured himself another glass. The walls sank into the earth, the floodlights went out, we were sitting in the open again.

Stüssi-Leupin stared straight ahead.

"My wife has been gracious enough to spare me the torture of attending her on her deathbed," he said, and it sounded indifferent. "That's why the priest was with her, and now the doctor and a nurse are in there. My wife, Spät, not only got one helluva kick out of life, rich as hell and Catholic as hell, she was a helluva beautiful woman. Strange, that use of 'hell.' She cheated on me all her life. The doctor sitting there with her was her last lover. But I understand her. A man like me is pure poison for women."

He laughed to himself, then abruptly changed the topic.

I was a fool, he said, I thought Isaak Kohler was guilty. He, Stüssi-Leupin, did too. True, all the witnesses contradicted one another; true, the murder weapon had never been found; true, there was no motive. Nevertheless. We thought he was guilty. Why? Because the murder had been committed in a crowded restaurant. Those who had been present had noticed the fact, one way or another, even though they now contradicted one another. And so we didn't know absolutely, but we believed absolutely. That had surprised him even at the trial. There had been no questions about the murder weapon, nor had witnesses been cross-examined, and the judge had been satisfied with the statement of the commandant, who had indeed been sitting close by but had not mentioned if he had seen the murder with his own eyes or if he had questioned witnesses—plus the defense lawyer was a dud, and Jämmerlin had been in top form. It would take all we could muster to reconcile our knowledge of Kohler's guilt with our belief in Kohler's guilt. Our knowledge stumbled along behind our belief, a clever defense lawyer could manufacture an acquittal on that discrepancy alone. But we really should give good old Jämmerlin the chance to come up with a motive. Kohler had thrown a lucrative job my way because I didn't understand anything about billiards. I had therefore drawn the conclusion—he had been listening carefully—that Kohler had killed in order to observe, to investigate, the laws of society, and had not admitted to such a motive precisely because the court would never have believed it. Dear friend, all he could say to that was that it was too literary a motive, the kind writers invent, even though he believed that with a man like Kohler it had to have been a very special motive. But of what sort?

Stüssi-Leupin pondered.

"You've drawn the wrong conclusion," he then said. "Because you don't understand anything about billiards. Kohler played *à la bande.*"

"*A la bande,*" I recalled. "That's what Kohler said to me once. While he was playing billiards at the Du Théâtre. '*A la bande.* That's how you have to beat Benno.'"

"And how did he play it?" Stüssi-Leupin asked.

"I don't rightly know." I thought back. "Kohler hit the ball to the edge, it ricocheted off and hit Benno's ball."

Stüssi-Leupin poured himself more wine.

"Kohler shot Winter in order to knock out Benno."

"But why?" I asked stupidly.

"Spät, you really are too naïve," Stüssi-Leupin said in amazement. "And here La Steiermann gave you the cue. Kohler manages her affairs. Even from prison. He's not just weaving baskets. Steiermann needs Kohler, and Kohler needs Steiermann, Lüdewitz is just window dressing. But who is the master, who the servant? Kohler's daughter has it right somehow. It was a murder done as a favor. Why not? And a kind of blackmail. Steiermann has her millions upon millions, but twenty million is still twenty million to her, and Kohler would have sensed that, and so he took out Benno by using Winter. Because Steiermann wished it. Perhaps she didn't even have to express the wish. Perhaps he just guessed it."

"An even crazier theory than the truth," I said. "Steiermann loved Benno because Daphne loved him, and only dumped him when Daphne left her."

"A more realistic theory than the truth, which is generally unbelievable," he countered.

"No one would accept your theory," I said.

"No one would accept the truth," he replied, "no judge, no jury, not even Jämmerlin. It's all played out on levels that are too high for the justice system to reach. The only theory that the courts will find plausible, when it comes to appeal, is that Dr. Benno is the murderer. Only he has a solid motive. Even if he's innocent."

"Even if he's innocent?" I asked.

"Does that bother you?" he replied. "His innocence is a theory too. He is the only one who could have got rid of the revolver. Dear friend, take over the appeal, and in a few years you'll be on a par with me."

The telephone rang. He picked it up, put it down.

"My wife is dead," he said.

"My condolences," I stammered.

"Don't mention it," he said.

He was about to pour himself more wine, but the bottle was empty. I stood up and poured him some of mine, setting the bottle down next to his.

"I'm driving," I said.

"I understand," he answered. "That Porsche must have cost a pretty penny."

I did not sit back down again. "I'm not going to take on the appeal, Herr Stüssi-Leupin, and I don't want to have anything more to do with this job. I'm going to destroy the results of the investigation," I declared.

He held his glass up to the floor lamp.

"How large was your advance?" he asked.

"Fifteen thousand and ten thousand for expenses."

A man with a bag came down the stairs, the doctor apparently, hesitated, trying to decide if he should come over to us, then the housekeeper appeared, led him out.

"You're going to have trouble paying that back," Stüssi-Leupin remarked. "And the total?"

"Thirty thousand plus expenses," I answered.

"I'll give you forty thousand, and you give me what you've found out."

I hesitated.

"You want to take on the appeal."

He was still gazing at his glass of red Talbot. "My business. Will you sell me the papers?"

"I suppose I have to," I replied.

He drank down his glass. "You don't have to, you want to." Then he refilled his glass, held it up to the light again.

"Stüssi-Leupin," I said and felt myself his equal, "if it comes to a trial, I'll be Benno's lawyer."

I left. As I moved into the shadow of one of the erratics, he called after me, "You weren't there, get that into your head, Spät, you weren't there, and I wasn't there either." Then he emptied his glass and fell back asleep.

... Dr.h.c. Isaak Kohler has notified me by telegram of his arrival: He will be landing on a flight from Singapore at 10:15 P.M., the day after tomorrow, and I will shoot him, and then shoot myself. So I have two nights left to finish my report. The announcement surprised me, maybe because I no longer believed he would ever come back. Granted, I am drunk. I was at the Höck, I'm always at the Höck of late, at one of the long wooden tables, among the other drunks. Been living off Giselle and the girls who've transferred here since the death of the Marquis, not from Neuchâtel, but from Geneva and Bern, while lots of the local girls have moved to Geneva or Bern, a considerable reorganization has been going on, which I personally have nothing to do with—can't do anything legally, or illegally, I've got nothing to do but wait until the day after tomorrow at 10:15 P.M. Orchid Noldi has taken over Lucky's old job, he's from Solothurn, they say, worked his way up in Frankfurt, and is very elegant, his girls are wearing orchids now; the police are furious, you can't outlaw orchids; a woman lawyer from Basel was crossing the street to the Bellevue at one in the morning with an orchid on her blouse—she was coming from a televised discussion about women's right to vote—she was arrested, didn't have an ID on her, a monumental scandal resulted; the police, the police spokesman, made fools of themselves—the latter by an inept démenti. Orchid Noldi is in absolute control, has brought Wicherten in as his lawyer, one of our best-regarded attorneys, who for reasons of social conscience has decided that he wants to defend the rights of such ladies—they pay taxes too, after all—and who advocates the introduction of massage parlors. Orchid Noldi indicated to me that, given my "lifestyle," I'm no longer considered tenable in the trade, but that he wouldn't dump me, he owed Lucky that much, he had consulted with his employees, as he put it, and for the time being I could stay on at the Höck; nor had the commandant bothered me again, no one seems interested in how Lucky and the Marquis met their end, and Daphne's mysterious death has been completely forgotten. So that, though I don't actually earn my living by pimping, I earn it by pumping. When the guests in the Höck ask me for addresses and I fork them over, free of charge, and then the guests—most elderly gentlemen—pay for my whiskey, well, that's just doing things with a certain style, just second nature. Which explains my intoxicated condition, my wretched handwriting, and my haste, because to be honest, when I found Kohler's telegram waiting for me, I went out on a binge, managed somehow to get back to Spiegelgasse, and here I sit, twenty hours later, at my desk. Luckily, and amazingly, I've still got a bottle of Johnnie Walker, but now I remember there was a dentist from Thun who looked me up at the Höck and whom I introduced to Giselle—I've just got back from the Monaco, not the Höck, as I've apparently implied—the haste with which I have to get all this down prevents me from either reading back over it or digressing from the point—I earned the bottle of Johnnie Walker; Giselle wasn't smitten by the dentist, gave her the willies, drinking his Veuve Clicquot—the second bottle—he took out his dentures, first the uppers and then the lowers, had made them himself, showed us his initials, *C.V.*, next to the upper left wisdom tooth, held the dentures in his hand, clattered away with them and tried to use them to bite Giselle's breast; at the next table, Hindelmann laughed till the tears dribbled down his belly, especially when the dentist dropped his dentures under the table, not under our table, but under Hindelmann's, where he was sitting with Marilyn, a new girl from Olten, which is where Orchid Noldi comes from too—no, he's from Solothurn—wait, maybe he is from Olten—so that the dentist had to go crawling on all fours looking for them, because no one wanted to pick them up but kept kicking them on to the next table. Finally Giselle decided she would after all, it had grown late, what with all our laughing, and I got my Johnnie Walker. What annoyed me about Hindelmann's whinnies was the absolutely wretched role he had played as part of the prosecuting team at Kohler's trial. Trial, not appeal. Everyone expected Stüssi-Leupin to steer the case to an appeal, but his petition to the Department of Justice was a surprise all the same. Dr.h.c. Isaak Kohler had never admitted that he had shot and killed Adolf Winter, professor of Germanics, in the Restaurant Du Théâtre. An eyewitness report was not sufficient if the defendant denied the charge; even an eyewitness could be mistaken. The Kohler case belonged therefore before a jury, not before the judges of a higher court. Therefore every juridical and legal means must be used to declare the old verdict invalid and to bring Kohler's case before a jury as it deserved. Stüssi-Leupin's position resulted first in a feverish ransacking of the case file and court records, which to the horror of the minister of justice, Moses Sprünglin, confirmed the fact that there had been no admission of guilt—people had simply regarded Kohler's philosophical flourishes as such; secondly, in the minister of justice's forcing Jegerlehner, the presiding judge of the appellate court, into an early retirement and his censuring the four other judges as well as Prosecutor Jämmerlin; and thirdly, in his handing the case over to a jury trial—a rash decision from a legal point of view. Jämmerlin's temper tantrum had no effect, his petition to the Supreme Court was denied with almost sensational speed, posthaste, so to speak—a unique achievement for an organ of government so overworked it normally moves at a snail's pace—in short, Kohler had his new trial by April of 1957.

Jämmerlin would not yield, he wanted to appear as the prosecutor once again, but Stüssi-Leupin objected that he was biased. Jämmerlin fought like Satan himself, and only yielded when he heard that Stüssi-Leupin was going to call Lienhard as one of his witnesses. To be sure, Feuser was no match for Stüssi-Leupin either—which reminds me I haven't yet given an account of the trial itself, nothing about the painful role the commandant played by declaring that he had not seen Kohler shoot, had merely assumed he had. Stüssi-Leupin pulled out all the stops. He was brilliant, I must admit. The witnesses he called so contradicted one another that the jury had to stifle their laughter and the audience simply squeaked with pleasure; Stüssi-Leupin played like a virtuoso on the theme of the revolver's never having been found, on the fact that since this had been passed over, the corpus delicti was therefore lacking, which was of itself sufficient basis for acquitting Kohler. Gradually, however, Stüssi-Leupin shifted suspicion to Benno, who at the time of the crime at the Du Théâtre had been the owner of a collection of revolvers—he was after all a Swiss master in pistol-shooting—which according to Lienhard he had tried to sell because of financial difficulties (a murmur passed through the courtroom); then followed intimations of a quarrel between Dr. Benno and Professor Winter, a cross-examination of Benno became unavoidable, everyone was anxiously awaiting his testimony, but Dr. Benno did not appear before the jury. I had been looking for him for days. I was determined to take over his defense, as I had told Stüssi-Leupin I would, and I badly needed information from Benno in order to investigate Kohler further, but even at the Sky-High Bar no one knew for sure.

Feuchting figured he was hiding out at Daphne's, she was a brick and wouldn't leave an old lover in the lurch; a certain Emil E., a deodorant salesman, who had dropped his last month's salary at her place on Aurorastrasse, had had the impression that someone else was in the apartment. But he still could not be located. People assumed he had fled. The police were notified, Interpol was called in, it was almost like Isaak Kohler's arrest. Daphne made things difficult, demanded a search warrant; but the next morning, as Ilse Freude entered my office on Zeltweg, she found the jaunty fencer and master pistol-shot dangling from the chandelier, swaying in the breeze between the door she had opened and the open window—Benno had kept a key to his old office and had climbed up on my desk, formerly his desk; all the while I had been over at Daphne's trying to track him down—for days I smelled of all sorts of perfumes, the ones that came from Emil E., the deodorant salesman… Maybe that's the reason that I have no stomach for reporting about the trial: If Stüssi-Leupin had cross-examined Daphne, my renewed relationship with Daphne would have come up, and that with Hélène present, and he surely would have done it, if Benno had not got the jump on him by committing suicide, which was interpreted as an admission of guilt. Dr.h.c. Isaak Kohler was acquitted with colors flying and trumpets blaring. As he was leaving the courtroom, he passed by me, stopped and regarded me with those cold, passionless eyes of his, and said that what had just gone on here had been the most wretched solution possible, that I had got myself into financial difficulty, well, my God, that was understandable, but why hadn't I come to him instead of handing over the investigative reports to

Stüssi-Leupin, who had then staged this ugly judicial production, an acquittal, for chrissake, it was embarrassing to have to stand there like an innocent lamb—who was all that innocent anyway? Then he said something that brought my anger to a white heat, made it clear to me that it was my duty to shoot Kohler down, because someone had to restore justice if all this was not to be an out-and-out farce: If only I had delivered the reports to him, he said, instead of selling them to Stüssi-Leupin, then Benno would have dangled from that chandelier without this silly trial, and then he gave me a poke as if I were a fellow scoundrel, sending me staggering into Mock, who was standing behind me and now pulled his hearing aid from his vest pocket and said, "Ah yes." Kohler left the courthouse. Victory celebration at the Ameise Guild House. Speech by the mayor in hexameters, then off to Australia, and I came running with my revolver, too late. Everybody knows the story. That was a year and a half ago, and now it's autumn again. It's always autumn. My God, drunk again, I'm afraid my handwriting will be unreadable, and it's eleven in the morning—another thirty-five hours and fifteen minutes—if I keep on boozing, there'll be a catastrophe. Damn, if Hélène still loved me, that would be like my own death sentence. I can only assure you that I loved her, love her still maybe, although she's sleeping with that old geezer Stüssi-Leupin, and not long ago I saw her with Friedli, he had his right arm around her shoulders, as if she had long ago become his property, but it's of no consequence really. It's not necessary for me to write about my conversation with Berger, the sect's preacher, on the stairs a while ago—a while ago, I was going back to the Höck for one last time, but it was a bust, couldn't rustle up any whiskey, the regulars were watching a soccer match and were in a bad mood because the Swiss were playing so badly, and the guys who normally asked me about addresses were in a bad mood too. The Monaco was closed. I didn't have any money on me, had forgotten my wallet, I had to have some whiskey, I staggered into the Du Théâtre, it was empty too; Alfredo, if it was Alfredo, gave me a strange look, Ella and Klara emerged resolutely from the background, someone called my name. Stüssi-Leupin was sitting at the table where James Joyce had always sat, and with a motion of his hand invited me to sit down with him. Ella and Klara didn't like to see this, but Stüssi-Leupin is Stüssi-Leupin. I should button up my fly, he suggested, and when I sat down, he remarked that I was letting myself go to hell, and poured some kirsch in his coffee. I needed a bottle of whiskey, I said, my mind elsewhere, my condition was hopeless, I realized that I couldn't live without whiskey, the panic-stricken fear overcame me that I wouldn't be able to get hold of any whiskey, while everything in me rebelled against drinking anything but whiskey, wine, say, or beer or schnapps or even the hard cider the clochards drink here (which is why they have bad livers but no rheumatism), some remnant of human dignity in me demanded that I drink only whiskey, for the sake of justice, which was destroying me, and there was Ella setting a glass in front of me. The Stüssi valley needed a lawyer again, Stüssi-Leupin said, his successor, the spokesman Stüssi-Sütterlin, had been shot during a hunt, someone had mistaken him for a chamois, either a Stüssi-Bierlin or a Stüssi-Feusi, or even a Stüssi-Moosi might have done it, the judge at the inquest in Flötigen had shelved the case, hopeless to try to solve it; that would be a job for me, I would be the first non-Stüssi to act as spokesman, and my readmission to the bar could be arranged. He was suggesting me of all people, I replied and chugged the whiskey; you of all people he replied, think about it, Spät, he went on, it was time for me to draw some conclusions, and if it was his, Stüssi-Leupin's, passion to save even the guilty from the jaws of that old shark the justice system, if there was a chance for them to escape the beast, to employ that particular metaphor, it wasn't because he wanted to make a fool of the justice system. A lawyer was not a judge: whether or not he believed in justice and in the laws deduced from that ideal was ultimately a matter of metaphysics, like the question about the nature of numbers, but the lawyer's task was to investigate whether some fellow whom the justice system had collared ought to be regarded as innocent or guilty, quite apart from the fact of whether he was guilty or not. Hélène had told him about my suspicion, but my investigation had been inadequate, Hélène had been a stewardess at the time—good God, in those days people still thought there was something special about the job—but not on the plane on which the English minister had flown back to his island. He had flown on a military plane and would hardly have made use of a Swissair stewardess. That Hélène had been so vague in her answer to my question that day was quite understandable, she hadn't understood the point of the question, and as far as what Kohler had had to say to me, which Mock had been reported to him, that was quite incomprehensible to him. Kohler had wanted a new trial; if he hadn't wanted to stand there like an angel of innocence all he would have had to do was declare he had gunned down his old PEN

Club brother and explain how, damn it all, he had managed to get rid of that revolver; he, Stüssi-Leupin, had a damned uneasy feeling; getting the old man acquitted had been his legal duty, but now it was dawning on him that he had let a beast loose, a lone wolf, the most dangerous sort; behind Kohler's crime there lay a motive that he wouldn't come clean about; at first he had thought that Steiermann was using Kohler, now it looked to him as if Kohler was using Steiermann. Winter, Benno, Daphne, the two pimps, a few too many corpses, and if I didn't pipe down, I might suddenly find myself being fished out of the Sihl. Well then, I had my bottle of whiskey, and I have no idea how I got back to Spiegelgasse—while Stüssi-Leupin had been dishing out his wisdom, Ella had provided the whiskey—that I've been able to record the conversation at all is a miracle, it's already one-thirty in the morning, I must have nodded off in the meantime– so a little more than twenty hours—nineteen hours, I read the clock wrong, it's two-thirty—and Kohler will—Dr.h.c. Kohler will—the conversation with Simon Berger must have taken place when I got back to Spiegelgasse with Stüssi-Leupin's whiskey. It must be weeks now since the psalms of the Latter-day Saints of Uetli died away, they suddenly ceased to resound—Stuber from vice had been visiting me, was dropping some pretty clear hints that the officials were still of the opinion that there was some connection between me and organized hookerdom, when the hymn "Jesus Christ, from Thy wounds bloody" broke off all of a sudden and was followed by the sound of screams, protests, howls, a most peculiar noise, and then the thunder of many feet moving down the stairs, then deadly silence, and Stuber went on with his guesswork: which was why I ought to have been amazed to find the preacher standing at the door of the sect's assembly room on the floor below me. He was leaning against the door, immobile, I tried to get by him, he tumbled on top of me. He would have fallen had I not caught him. As I pushed him away from me, I saw that his face was badly burned and his eyes were missing. Horrified, I tried to move on up the stairs, to my room, but Berger wouldn't let go of me, he clasped me in his arms and shouted that he had stared into the sun to gaze upon God, and when he had seen God he had gained his sight, he once was blind but now could see, he could see, and screaming this, he tugged at me so that we both ended up lying on the stairs leading up to my room. I don't know what all he told me, I was too drunk to comprehend it, it was probably nonsense, all those babblings about the sun's interior, the total darkness that reigned there, which at the same time was the hiddenness of God, which you can recognize only when you let the sun burn away your eyes, only then did you perceive how God was submerged inside the sun as a dimensionless point of perfect blackness, sucking the sun into Himself with an endless thirst, without ever growing larger, as if He were a bottomless hole, the abyss of abysses, and how the sun was emptying itself into its interior, and thus was expanding, no one noticed it as yet, but tomorrow night at ten-thirty it would happen, the sun, having become pure light, would burst into rays and expand at the speed of light, scorching everything, the earth would evaporate in a huge aura of light; that's the gist of it, he talked like a drunk to a drunk, which I was at the time and am even drunker now and don't know why I'm writing about this sectarian preacher, who stood up in front of his congregation with his head all wrapped up, declared the end of the world, and demanded that his followers should let their eyes be burned out by the sun as his had been, and then ripped the veil away: the screams, protests, howls, that most peculiar noise I had heard, the congregation thundering down the stairs—that had been his answer. Have read back over what I've written. About three hours now until I have to leave for the airport. The commandant must have got here at seven-thirty this morning, maybe even before that, he was sitting right in front of my couch, I was amazed to see him sitting there when I awoke, which is to say, I only noticed him after I had thrown up and was returning from the toilet, tried to lie back down on the couch. The commandant asked if he should make some coffee, then without waiting for my answer went over to the kitchenette, I fell asleep again, and when I came to, the coffee was ready, we drank it in silence. Did I know, the commandant then asked, that I was one in ten, and when I asked what his strange question meant, he replied that he let every tenth person go and that I was one of those. Otherwise he would have had to arrest me beside Daphne's grave; like myself he had been a lawyer, even less successful than I, employed only now and again as a public defender, and so he had ended up with the police; he was a socialist and his friends in the party, who would never have dreamed of turning to him if they had had personal need of a lawyer, had fixed him up with a job in the criminal division of the municipal police, as the legal advisor; that he had slid his way to the top and ended up as commandant had not been the result of any special achievement, political intrigue had washed him up onto those higher shores, and it was the same with the other levels of the justice system; not that he meant to imply that there was corruption, but the claim by the justice system to represent something objective, some sort of sterilized instrument free of every social bias and prejudice, was so far from being the real state of affairs that he could not regard the Kohler case as tragically as I; to be sure, I had made the mistake of taking on the commission and of handing the reports over to Stüssi-Leupin, which resulted in Kohler's being able to harass Benno to death-by-chandelier and win his retrial, but—regardless of whether Kohler was innocent or not—and everyone knew after all that the canton deputy had shot and killed the university professor, even he, the commandant, had no doubts of that—when he looked at me now and considered the mess I had got myself into by rebelling against an acquittal, which, though juridically speaking most remarkable, was itself incontestable and thus perfectly justified—even if it had put justice in checkmate—then I had no choice, if I wanted to see justice done in this affair, but to condemn Kohler and myself to death and to carry out the death sentence on us both, to take the revolver that I had kept hidden behind my couch and use it to dispatch Kohler and then myself into the next world; all of which he, the commandant, considered quite logical, but also quite absurd, because before justice—taken as an absolute, which after all it was, in the ideal sense—I was no better off than Kohler, he needed to remind me only of the role I played in Daphne's death. Before justice, Kohler and I stood face to face as two murderers. By comparison, a judge performed a perfectly acceptable service. He had to see to the proper functioning of an imperfect institution, which the justice system admittedly was, taking care that the rules of the human game were observed at least to some extent. A judge no more needed to be a just man himself than the pope needed to be a believer. But whenever someone took it upon himself to execute justice, things got damned inhuman. Such a fellow overlooked the fact that sometimes swindling was more human than propriety, because the world's gears needed to be greased from time to time, a task for which our nation seemed to have a particular knack. Such a fanatic of justice must himself be a just man, and he would leave it to me whether I was that or not. You see, Commandant, I am quite capable of recording our conversation—or better, your lecture, since I didn't say a word, just lay there, soiled with vomit, and listened to you—with at least tolerable accuracy as to the gist of it; nor was I at all astonished that you had guessed what I decided from the very beginning I was going to do; and maybe that's why I let myself go to the dogs, possibly that's why I helped Lucky and the Marquis from Neuchâtel with their alibi, apparently that's why I've become what I am, too shabby for even an Orchid Noldi and beneath the dignity of the ladies he represents—all of it for only one reason: so that I could be just as guilty as Dr.h.c. Isaak Kohler, for then my sentence and my executing that sentence upon myself are as just as anything in the world, because justice can only be executed among those who are equally guilty; just as there is only one crucifixion, the one on the Isenheim Altar, a crucified giant hangs on the cross, a ghastly corpse, beneath whose weight the beams to which he is nailed sag, a Christ even more dreadful than those for whom this altar was painted, for lepers; when they saw that God hanging there, justice was established between them and the God who, so they believed, had sent leprosy upon them: This God had been justly crucified for them. I'm sober as I write this, Herr Prosecutor Feuser, I'm sober as I write this, and for precisely that reason I beg you not to reprimand the commandant for not taking away my revolver; our entire conversation, or better, the commandant's entire straight-arrow lecture was not intended to be fatherly; that stuff about every tenth person that he lets go—whoever wants to believe that, well let them—but he'd probably be only too glad if he could catch every tenth criminal, the whole thing was meant as a provocation. He was mad at himself afterward for not having arrested me at the funeral, when the umbrella flew off and he took the stiletto from my hand; but I know him, he thinks fast, he understood that not only would the question of who murdered Daphne Müller have had to be reopened but also the question of who had murdered the murderers, and he would then have found himself in Monika Steiermann's domain, and who wants to pick a fight with a prosthesis empire that's about to get back into the arms business; but when two hours from now—more precisely, two hours and thirty minutes from now—I take my shot at Dr.h.c. Isaak Kohler, the commandant will jump in, even if the shots have no effect—oh yes, Herr Prosecutor, let's agree to this much: First of all, the commandant with his touching lecture was trying to ensure that those shots, if I was going to shoot, would not be dangerous; but you had no way of knowing, Herr Commandant (I'm addressing you again now), that I had long ago exchanged the blanks for real bullets. Which is why I never went into detail about the secondhand shop on the ground floor. Pure instinct. So that *you* wouldn't go into detail about it. The one-eyed fellow who ran it was quite a character, you could find everything in there. Was. For that's all past now, the secondhand dealer moved out three weeks ago, his store on the ground floor is empty, as is his first-floor apartment, and everything is silent and deserted among the Saints of Uetli, and yesterday (or the day before, or the day before that) I also found a registered letter that I received months ago but never read, informing me that the house on Spiegelgasse, while a landmark building, is in total disrepair and in desperate need of renovation, that the latter is to be undertaken by Friedli, who will gut the inside and build luxury apartments in the old frame, his newest enterprise, and that I am to vacate my apartment by October 1st, and since October 1st has long since passed, I've had to wander around town trying to scare up my last bottle of whiskey, came up with it at some point, yesterday, from Stüssi-Leupin at the Du Théâtre, otherwise I would have scared up a bottle in the apartment of the one-eyed secondhand dealer, not whiskey but a bottle of grappa, the same way I found the bullets in his shop, in the bell of an alpine horn, and then tossed in the blanks with which you, Herr Commandant, had loaded my revolver. Dr.h.c. Isaak Kohler and I will die to the strains of Swiss folk music. But before I—even though sobriety threatens me more and more, like some sun rising up before me into which, like the mad preacher, I am forced to stare—before I drive out to the airport in less than an hour (in my VW, it didn't survive its repairs all that well, meaning, I didn't let them finish, lack of funds), I have one last word for you, Commandant: I retract my suspicion. You acted correctly. You wanted to allow me the freedom of my decision, did not want to compromise my dignity. I am sorry that I have decided differently from what you hoped. And now a final confession: In my game of justice, I have gambled not only myself away but Hélène as well, the daughter of the man whom I shall murder, and who is my murderer. I shall shoot myself because I shall have shot him. Futurum exactum. I remember now the Latin lessons an old pastor gave me at the orphanage, preparing me for high school in the city. I've always liked talking about the orphanage, I even told Mock about it, although it was difficult to carry on a conversation with him. Once, when a writer was telling us about the death of his mother, to whom he apparently had been quite devoted, I began to explain the advantages of the orphanage and described the family as the breeding place of crime, saying that all this constant praise of familial happiness made me want to vomit, which visibly annoyed the writer, but Mock just laughed, though with him one never knew what he was getting from a conversation and what he was missing—if as usual he had misplaced his hearing aid, he could read lips, or so I assume, though he disputes this (another one of his tricks), but my bragging about having grown up without father or mother, he said, gave him an eerie feeling, but fortunately, he continued in his fussy way—the writer had long since departed—I had become a lawyer and had no plans to become a politician, although that was always still a possibility, but a man who waxed enthusiastic about an orphanage was worse than someone who spent his youth quarreling with his father or mother or with both, as he, Mock, had, who had loathed his old man and old lady, as he put it, although they had both been the soul of Christian kindness, but he had hated them because they had conceived eight children plus himself, without ever asking a single member of that excessively numerous squad of children whether he or she wanted to be born, conception was a crime without parallel; whenever he chiseled furiously away at some lump (he meant one of his stones), he always imagined that he was taking his revenge on either his father or his mother, but in my case he had to ask what sort of person I was with this orphanage mania of mine. Fine, he, Mock, had hate in his belly for those who had conceived him, had given him birth, and then hadn't swept him up into the next garbage can, and he was hewing that hate out of stone into a figure, into a form that he loved because he had created it, and that, if it could feel, would hate him in turn, just as he had hated the parents who had loved him, whose problem child he had been; all of which was only human, a cycle of hate and love between creator and creation, but when, in comparison, he tried to imagine someone like me, who instead of hating those who gave him life, instead of hating life itself, loved an institution that had brought him forth and trained him, and who therefore was predestined to spawn a passion for the nonhuman, for an ideology, or for just a single principle, for justice, to take an example, and then when he went on to imagine how such a person would deal with those fellow humans who did not live up to his principle of justice, staying with that example (and who could ever live up to it really?), it made him break out in a sweat of purest anxiety. His hate was productive, mine destructive, the hate of a murderer. "Good God, Spät," he concluded his barely comprehensible line of reasoning, "I feel sorry for you. You're damned screwed-up." After which I never entered his studio again. Why am I telling you about this conversation, Herr Commandant? Because this sculptor, currently being lionized in Venice, is right as hell. I am a test-tube human, bred in a model laboratory, raised according to the principles of the pedagogues and psychiatrists that our nation has produced along with precision watches, psychopharmaceuticals, secret bank accounts, and eternal neutrality. I would have been a model product of this experimental institute, except that I lacked one thing: a billiard table. Thus I was placed into the world without being able to see through it—because I had never come to grips with it, because I imagined it was governed by the rules of the orphanage in which I grew up. Quite unprepared, I was cast into the system in which humans prey upon one another; quite unprepared, I saw myself confronted by the instincts that form them, greed, hate, fear, cunning, the thirst for power, but I was equally helpless when subjected to the feelings that make that predatory system humane: dignity, moderation, reason, and, ultimately, love. I was swept away from human reality like a nonswimmer in a raging river; struggling not to perish, I myself became a beast of prey as I perished, to whom came—after my conversation that night with Stüssi-Leupin, during which I sold him the materials that would serve to acquit a murderer—the murderer's daughter: Hélène was waiting for me in my law office on Zeltweg, in the posh, roomy apartment that I had taken over from Benno. Only now am I struck by the fact that she was waiting for me in my apartment, not at the door. In the armchair in front of my desk. And that she knew her way around inside. But then Benno—who hadn't fallen for him? She came because she trusted me, and so she surrendered herself because I desired her, but I lacked the courage to trust her as well, failed to believe she desired me because she loved me. And so our love failed. I did not tell her that her father had not been forced to murder (even if that infernal dwarf may have wanted it), that he was simply taking pleasure in playing God on this wretched planet of ours, and that I had sold myself twice over, once to him and once to a star lawyer who took his pleasure in letting the game of justice be played out, like a master who magnanimously takes over in a chess game that a novice has begun. And so we slept together, without speaking to each other, unaware that there is no happiness without speech. Which is perhaps why the only real happiness is momentary, like the happiness I sensed that night as I became aware of what could have become of me, of a possibility beyond my grasp, which lay within me but which I had not actualized, and because I was happy then, for one whole night long, I was convinced that I would become what I did not become. When we stared at each other the next morning, we knew it was all over. Now I have to get to the airport.

III

Editor's Afterword: By truly strange coincidence, I made the acquaintance of several persons who, as I only later realized, were not only involved in this multilayered story but had indeed also played the principal roles in it.

It must have been around 1984. In Munich. I don't keep a diary. My dates and times are never all that exact. I assume toward the end of May, and at the time I considered the whole story to be pure fabrication. A comfortable villa, a comfortable park receding beneath tall trees. In the park, along one side of the villa, tables have been laid. A pleasant hostess. Publishers, journalists, neatly measured doses from the world of film, theater, culture. As always, I mistake someone for someone else. Am uncertain whether some other woman is the same woman I assume she is. And in fact she turns out to be someone else. Then some other man is somebody totally different. In my fright, I frighten a director of a theater where I once knew everyone and now don't know anyone. I think, he thinks I'm trying to palm a play off on him, and he thinks I'm trying to palm a play off on him. An actor is running around like a King Lear who has forgotten his lines and is inconsolable: "The theater is done for. There aren't any new plays." There's another actor whom I've seen so often on television that I imagine he's an old acquaintance, and he is bewildered, because this is the first time we've met. A woman arrives shoving an old man in a wheelchair. Elegant, self-confident, beautiful. Around fifty. I recognize her but don't know her name. She greets me with reserve, uses the informal pronoun and calls me Max. She has mistaken me for someone else. Laughter. She apologizes. I feel honored. She goes back to formal address. Who was the old man? Her father. He has to be ancient. Close to a hundred. Delicate and fragile. Uncommonly animated. Pink skin. Thin white hair, trimmed moustache, well-groomed beard, full but shaped to a goatee. He has just come from a conference with the prime minister of Bavaria. About politics? About a foundation for effective science. I don't understand. There is too much useless science around these days. I understand. She still thinks I know her, and I don't. Our hostess is talking with the old man. Small talk. Laughs a lot. The old man must be witty. I sit down between the acquaintance I'm unacquainted with and the German widow of an Italian publisher, whom I once got to know during a day in Milan. The acquaintance whose name I can't come up with has noticed that I don't know who she is. She is dumbfounded. The widow is talking to me about an actress with whom I was once in love. She ran off with a fire-man. After our meal, into the drawing room. The film and theater folk flock around the director. They are interested in art. The others around the old man in the wheelchair. They are interested in reality. An art critic holds the two spheres together for a few minutes with a speech thanking our host-ess. He knows too much about art not to underestimate reality, and too much about reality not to overestimate art. Then the two spheres fall apart again. Some of them are discussing

Botho Strauss, others Franz Josef Strauss. What did the old man think of the latter? Historian, not a meteorologist. What did he mean by that? The historian made long-term predictions. He was a metaphysician. Imagined that he had a handle on the *Weltgeist*. The meteorologist dared no more than short-term predictions. He was a scientist. Did not imagine he had a handle on our capsule of gas. The world was too opaque. What was politically possible? Quick surgical measures, and then observe the accidental effects. What did he mean by that? A firm that he had once voluntarily advised and had involuntarily managed had found itself in a difficult position. It was unnecessary to go into detail. Economic interrelationships were even more complicated than a capsule of gas, the predictions even less precise. The old man spoke easily, softly and quickly. Only now and then was there a noticeable soft clatter of dentures. It had merely revolved around the necessity of murdering someone or of having him murdered. Everyone was dumbfounded. Embarrassed. But then touched somehow. As if the old man were going to tell a love story. To be sure, broaching the topic of murder was a faux pas. Even the culture group lent an ear. It was almost as if the old man had eaten his fish with his knife. But kings and almost-centenarians are allowed to do that, too. "He's simply charming," an actress said, breathing heavily in our direction; I had seen her, or thought I had, on television or in a film. The screen and the tube bake faces into pastry. At least ten of them look alike. The old man accepted a glass of champagne. He sipped. A film director and actor, whom I had known for a long time, appeared. Of Swiss origin. The Russian-prince type, after the loss of his estates, accustomed to associating with serfs. Large, portly, his beard well-groomed, dressed with casual care. Kissed the hostess's hand, noticed the puzzled guests, passed over them in amusement, said with his unique heartwarming grandezza, "Hello, Herr Canton Deputy, hello, Hélène," waved to me, not ungraciously, then said, "I see our canton deputy is about to tell his story. It's fantastic," poured himself a glass of champagne, sat down. The old man went on with his story. He exuded an authority that held everyone in his sway. It was not a matter of what he said, but of how he said it. And so it is quite impossible to reproduce the story as he told it. He hoped his hostess would forgive him for having spoken of murder so bluntly. Someone had asked him what was politically possible, he continued, or to that effect. Politics and business were governed by the same laws, the laws of power. That applied to war as well. In particular, business was a continuation of war by other means. As there were wars between nations, so there were wars between corporations. Civil wars corresponded to the internal struggles within a corporation. One was faced on all sides with the necessity of either excluding someone from power or of being excluded oneself. Which demanded a quick surgical measure, and that one then wait to see if it was successful or not. It required, he admitted, only in the rarest instances that murder be committed. Murders are actually ineffectual measures. Terrorism ruffles only the surface of the world's structure. His murder had been necessary. But it was not murder that had been the problem, but the realization that only murder could help. Certainly he could have ordered the murder committed. All tasks could be delegated. But he would soon be a hundred and had always tied his own shoes till now. Should further murders prove necessary later on, they would take care of themselves, God had reached out only once to create the world. One nudge would suffice. And the solution to his problem had come to him like a bolt of lightning. He smirked. Over thirty years ago now, he had had to accompany a politician, a man as famous as he was disliked, from a private clinic to the airport. At the clinic, the famous politician had stood beside his bed wrapped in confusion and a thick winter coat. He was being followed. The inheritance tax he had got passed in parliament had ruined too many people. He would have to defend himself. He pulled a revolver from his pocket. He would use it to kill every disinherited heir. A nurse had rushed off screaming for help. Then he had stuck the revolver back in his pocket. The doctor came racing in with two aides. A colonel in the military, a crude man of medicine, whose diagnosis was that the illness had now invaded the politician's brain as well, ah well, not all that bad in his profession, he'd simply pump his man full of tranquilizers, then send him on his way home, otherwise he might kick the bucket right here. After a brief struggle, during which one aide was knocked out, the poor fellow was relieved of his winter coat, revolver included, he was given a rear end—the ladies would excuse him—full of shots, packed back into his winter coat, and stuffed into his Rolls-Royce. And so he had driven into town with an armed, and crazy, statesman. A magnificent spring evening. Just as darkness fell. Around seven. Since his countrymen arose early, they dined early. While he was driving down Rämistrasse with the dozing genius of government finance at his side and watching people rush to get into the restaurants, there popped into his head a possible method for solving his problem in the most elegant manner. "My God," said the German widow of the Italian publisher, "this is exciting." The person, the old man went on, whose influence in the firm he had to eliminate was in the habit of dining at this hour in a very well known restaurant. The old man emptied his second glass of champagne. He had the driver stop, removed the revolver from the coat pocket of the softly snoring minister, made certain that he had guessed correctly and that the person in question was on the premises, whereupon he shot him and, back in the Rolls-Royce now, returned the revolver to the politician's coat pocket and drove Her Majesty's honorable minister out to the airport and loaded him on a special flight, which had then lifted the ailing party leader and his revolver through the air to his island, where no sooner had he arrived than he brought the former world empire to final financial ruin. Soft giggles from the culture section. The daughter maintained a ghostly, majestic calm. Her father could have related that he had been in charge of a concentration camp, and she wouldn't have batted an eye. But we were all listening spellbound. As if to an old bomb-thrower. And yet amused, even delighted, charmed, by the ease and irony with which the old man told his tale, shifting it all into something abstract, unreal. A publisher asked in confusion: "And you?"—"My good man," the old man replied, extracting a fat cigar from an etui (I would guess, remembering my own smoking days, that it was a Topper), "my good man," he was forgetting two things. The social circles in which we moved, and the justice system, which, though perhaps more unconsciously than consciously, accommodated itself to whatever social circle it was to render a decision about, even though—especially in regard to members of the privileged class—it would sometimes proceed all too frenetically in an attempt to deny the prejudices which it in fact did have. But why should he bore us. He was arrested, sentenced by an appellate court, but then acquitted by a jury, despite the fact that the murder had taken place in full public view. Well, you see, necessity demanded it. Several pieces of evidence were missing. The witnesses contradicted one another. The murder weapon was never found. Who was going to look in a minister's coat? They hadn't been able to prove he had a motive. A corporation is a shadow world for a prosecutor. And then quite by chance, a Swiss world master in pistol-shooting had been present, who, when they tried to interrogate him, had hanged himself; one simply needed good luck, it was of course also possible that the fellow had shot at the very moment that he, he was seventy years old at the time, had been about to shoot; but the reality was a dead man, with his head lying in his tournedos rossini and green beans, as he recalled, and how this reality had come about was ultimately a secondary matter. He lit the cigar with which he had been playing, a little like a conductor with his baton. Suddenly the guests broke into laughter, several of them clapped, a fat journalist opened a window and laughed out into the night: "A joke to beat all." All of them were convinced of his innocence. Including me. Why, really? Because of his charm? His age? Delicious, the German widow of the Italian publisher beamed; our hostess remarked that life writes the most improbable tales; the daughter regarded me, coldly, attentively, as if trying to determine if I believed the story. The old man smoked his cigar and managed a trick I never could, he blew smoke rings. He understood, he said, that an innocently accused man was not as embarrassing as a murderer, and thus the hearty applause, it was his fate that no one wanted to believe he had committed a murder. Nor, he assumed—and he turned to me as he said it—did I believe him, though in writing my comedies I sent my heroes off into eternity by the truckload. Renewed laughter, people were having a great time, strong coffee was served, cognac. All that was left, the old man began once more, while concentrating on the ash of his cigar, which he had not knocked off but was carefully allowing to grow, was the moral question. Suddenly he was a different person. No longer a hundred years old but timeless. Whether he had killed or had only intended to kill, he said, in moral terms it was the intent that counted, not the execution. Yet the moral question was a question of justifying an act that did not correspond to the general principles of a society that ostensibly was governed by such principles. Thus the justification could be categorized as a dialectical one. Everything can be justified dialectically, and thus morally as well. Which was why he considered every justification a matter of bad style, or to overstate it, every morality immoral; he could only note that he had acted in the best interest of the corporation, which went bankrupt all the same, by the way, so that even his lovely murder had proved useless, whether he had committed it or someone else had, which then allowed one to answer the question of what was politically possible: If at all, then purely by accident, and, when something is achieved by accident, it represents the opposite of what one wanted to achieve. Then he offered his apologies. Our gracious hostess would be so kind as to excuse him and allow his daughter, Hélène, to take him to the Vier Jahreszeiten. She rolled him out without so much as a glance my way. I considered the story to be a fabrication. Who commits murder that way? But that the old man had once been powerful and had had considerable influence was not to be overlooked, why else would Strauss have received him? I thought of him as a business mogul who had his skeletons in the closet, but maneuvers on the market make for more complicated tales than murders, and so he had chatted away about a fabricated murder, which he could be sure that people would not think him capable of, in contradistinction to market speculations. No sooner was I in my taxi than I had forgotten his story and was pondering nothing more than the dialectic under which he had ordered morality, when suddenly I remembered his name: Kohler, Isaak Kohler. I had dined across from him once at a banquet given for the Friends of the Schauspielhaus. Next to him his daughter. At some point. Many years ago. I don't recall what the occasion for the celebration was. Endless speeches. Kohler sat there that night looking tanned and robust; his daughter remarked that he had just returned from a trip around the world.

The following summer, already early September perhaps. The father of an acquaintance had died, a Stüssi-Moosi. She had been our housemaid about fifteen years before. She sent me word that her father's farm was up for sale. I knew the farm. It was old and half fallen down. I was determined to buy it. An impressive view. Below, the Stüssi valley with the village of Stüssikofen, then Flötigen, the high Alps. Behind the farm a bluff fell steeply away. The village was a wide place in the road, still not in the real Alps. Old houses. A chapel. Now and again the pastor from Flötigen would preach. An inn. How astonishing that there still are villages without tourists. I was to deal with the "spokesman," which is what they call a lawyer there. He lived in a room of the inn Zum Leuenberger, taking care of business in the taproom. With farmers for an audience. He seemed to be more the village judge, was smoothing over a brawl as I arrived. A cursing farmer with a bandaged head was on his way out. With the passing of time, I find it difficult to describe the spokesman. Approaching his fifties. He might have been considerably younger. A chronic alcoholic. Drank *bäzi*, a kind of schnapps distilled from assorted fruits. He looked sort of hunchbacked, but wasn't. Peevish. The face bloated, not ignoble. The eyes watery blue, bloodshot. Crafty, for the most part, often dreamy. He tried to swindle me. He demanded double the price my former housemaid had indicated. Had some complicated story about difficulties with the Stüssikofen village council. He babbled on about unwritten laws. He claimed the farm was haunted, Stüssi-Moosi, the farmer, had hanged himself. Every Stüssi-Moosi farmer hanged himself. The farmers eavesdropped with brazen candor, mimed hanging when he mentioned farmers hanging themselves, put their right hands above their heads as if pulling on ropes, rolled their eyes, stuck out their tongues. I realized the spokesman was not trying to swindle me, but rather to prevent the farm from being sold—and then later on he swindled the family of our former housemaid. He sold the house for a song to a Stüssi-Sütterlin. Once he sensed that my interest in the farm was fading, owing more to the hostility of the farmers than to his subterfuges, he turned affable. Though of course he was also drunk by then. But not unpleasantly so. On the contrary. He began to be witty. Though in a vicious sort of way. He started to tell stories. The farmers moved in closer. They egged him on. Apparently they knew his stories. They listened to him the way people listen to someone telling fairy tales. He claimed he had been a famous lawyer in our nation's largest city. Had made money hand over fist. Worked for major banks, for the city's rich families. But his favorite clients had been the prostitutes. "My whores," as he phrased it. He had countless wild stories. Especially about a fellow named Orchid Noldi. I assumed he made most of them up. But I was fascinated.

Less by the stories themselves than by the social criticism he packed them with. There was something anarchic about them. They corresponded not to reality but to his own brain. He got tangled up in a story about a murder trial. He imitated the defendant, the five judges. The farmers whinnied. He had won the trial as the lawyer for the defense. And then he declared that the acquitted man had been the murderer after all. The acquitted man, a canton senator, had hoodwinked him and the five judges. The farmers hooted, they were drinking *bäzi* now too. They had obviously heard this story many times and couldn't get enough of it. They kept asking for the spokesman to go on, he played coy, they poured him some *bäzi,* he pointed at me, it wouldn't interest me, he was sure, they poured me some *bäzi,* of course, of course, it would interest me. The spokesman told how he had tried to have the case retried, but the government and ultimately the supreme court had prevented it. A canton senator was a canton senator after all. Every legal hurdle, every trick, evoked peals of mocking laughter. That's the way things were in free

Switzerland, a farmer shouted and ordered another *bäzi.* And so he had done it his way, the spokesman said. He had waited until the councillor had returned from a trip around the world. He had learned the arrival time from the newspapers. Then he had told the police commandant what he intended to do. Who had then had the airport sealed off. But the spokesman had smuggled his way in, disguised as a cleaning lady in the cleaning crew. He had hidden a revolver in his detachable artificial breasts. A policeman had made a grab for his falsies. The spokesman had screamed that he was being raped. The police commandant had apologized and had the cop locked up in the airport jail cell. The farmers slapped their thighs and yowled. Then the spokesman told how he had shot and killed the murderer whom he had helped get acquitted. On the way to the first-class lounge. The senator had fallen face first into a cleaning bucket. He had done in the 'scallion just like Tell had done in Gessler on the path through the gorge, a farmer bawled out. The others shouted their approval. One helluva racket. That was real justice. The spokesman acted out his arrest. Described how the commandant had ripped his falsies right off his body. Climbed up on the table. Held his defense summation before the five judges who had acquitted the murdered man and now had to acquit his murderer. He had told those judges they could "go to hell with their justice system" and had become the spokesman for the Stüssi valley. Then he fell off his chair. A farmer, a half-full bottle of *bäzi* in his left hand, helped him up, pounded the story teller on the shoulders, declared that he himself was a Stüssi-Stüssi, and the spokesman was the only non-Stüssi in Stüssikofen, but a Swiss to the bone for all that, then he chugged what was left in the bottle and fell across the table, began to snore. The others struck up the former national anthem, whose first verse ends with: "Hail, O Helvetia! Sons hast thou e'en yet, like those Saint Jacob met, joyful in war." The story seemed somehow familiar. I wanted to learn some further details, but the spokesman was too drunk for me to talk to him. Several of the farmers had stood up menacingly while the others were now singing the end of the second verse: "And should the Alps one day, e'er fail to guard the way, stand then with God, and like the very rock we'll stand inured to shock, death itself we mock, by pain unawed." I felt sorry for the spokesman. A star lawyer had ended up a down-at-the-heel backwoods pettifogger. He had committed a murder, had won his own trial, but the murder had finished him. I gave up the idea of buying the farm. I had to leave; in Stüssi valley there's no love lost for city people, and since they could see by my car that I was from Neuchâtel, I was a no-good outsider, although I could speak the same language they did, though perhaps sing it less. I left the inn. "When thou walkest into light, bathed in rays of morning bright, upon the height behold thy might! When the Alpine snows turn pink, but think, O Swiss, but think, ye have now seen and scanned God in his high Fatherland!" rumbled behind me. They had switched to the new national anthem.

Then forgotten again. The old man in the wheelchair, his daughter, the drunken murderer in the Stüssikofen taproom surrounded by drunken farmers—they sank into my unconscious. My annoyance at not having been able to buy the farm concealed them. It wasn't just on a whim that I had wanted to buy the farm. I needed a change. Back home again, I began to reorganize. Trash that had collected during forty years of writing and authoring was tossed away. Piles of unanswered correspondence, bills I had never seen and yet paid nevertheless, accounts I had never paid attention to, mountains of galleys, endless reworked manuscripts, fragments, photographs, drawings, caricatures, one helluva mess, some of which had to be put in order, some done away with. Mountains of unread manuscripts, submerged for decades in the flood of unanswered mail—I opened one at random. "The Execution of Justice." Pitch the rubbish. As I was throwing it away, my eyes fell on the first page of the manuscript, and I read the name Dr.h.c. Isaak Kohler. I retrieved the manuscript from its plastic bag. A certain Dr. H. had sent it from Zürich, but I never read manuscripts people send me. I'm not interested in literature, I write my own. Dr. H.—I tried to recall. Chur, 1957. After a lecture. In a hotel. I went to the bar to have a last whiskey. Besides the elderly woman tending bar, there was a gentleman, who introduced himself to me as soon as I had taken my seat. It was Dr. H., the former commandant of the canton police of Zürich, a large and heavyset man, old-fashioned, with a gold watch chain across his vest, the sort you seldom see nowadays. Despite his age, his bristly hair was still black, his moustache bushy. He was sitting on a high bar stool drinking red wine, smoking a Bahianos, and he addressed the woman tending bar by her first name. His voice was loud and his gestures were quite lively, a man with no affectations, who at once both attracted and frightened me. He drove me back to Zürich in his car the next morning. I paged through the manuscript. It had been typed. Above the title, handwritten: "Do what you want with this." I began to read the manuscript. I read it through. The author, a lawyer, was no match for his material. The present kept interfering. He waited till the end to tell the most important part, and then all at once he ran out of time. He hurried it. For the most part the work of a dilettante. And certain scenes disconcerted me, too. And then the chapter headings: an attempt to bring order to disorder. And some of the names. Who has a name like Nikodemus Molch, or Daphne Müller, or Ilse Freude? And who keeps a whole army of garden gnomes? Hadn't the commandant remarked that he loved Jean Paul? I couldn't ask the commandant. He had died. 1970. Then I read the letter the commandant had enclosed: "Just back from Stüssi-Leupin's funeral. Only Mock was there. Joined him at the Du Théâtre, ate liver dumpling soup, tournedos rossini with green beans. Afterward a long search for Mock's hearing aid. The waitress had carried it out on the platter. As far as our justice fanatic goes, he really did manage to sneak into the airport. As part of the cleaning crew. And he fired the shot too, and was so frightened when the gun went off that he fell face first into his bucket; fortunately Kohler didn't notice a thing, a four-engine job was just taking off. The assassin couldn't have done any damage in any case. He was wrong. I had checked out the secondhand dealer. The bullets in the alpine horn were carefully prepared blanks. Afterward didn't know what I should do with our justice fanatic. He was at the end of his tether. I didn't want to hand him over to the courts. Stüssi-Leupin (see above) took him on. Got him a job. That was several years ago. Your Dr. H., Commandant Emeritus." I placed a call to Stüssikofen. The keeper of the inn Zum Leuenberger answered. I asked for the spokesman. Dead. "Pegged out" last week. What had they called him? Called him? Spokesman. Where was he buried? In Flötigen, he thought. I drove there. The cemetery lay outside of town. Enclosed by a stone wall. A wrought-iron entrance gate. It was cold. The first time I had sensed winter coming on that year. Something about cemeteries makes me feel at home. I played in a cemetery as a child. It had individuality. Every dead person had his own grave, you saw gravestones, wrought-iron crosses, pedestals, columns, even an angel. On the grave of one Christeli Möser. But the Flötigen cemetery was a modern cemetery, a cemetery ratified by the Flötigen town council ten years before. Whatever had died previously was no longer to be found. Since the cemetery's size was limited and could not be expanded—the price of land was too high—only ten years' rest in local soil was allowed. Then off to eternity. But during those ten years, you had to lie nice-and-proper-like. Each in a grave like every other. With the same flowers. The same gravestone. Chiseled with the same script. And so the dead lay in ordered ranks, even the one I was looking for. Disorderly in life, orderly as a corpse. The last one, next to a still-empty grave. The stone and the flowers (asters, chrysanthemums) were already in place. On the gravestone:

FELIX SPÄT, SPOKESMAN, 1930–1984

Back home again, I read the manuscript through once more. It must have been a typed copy of the original. Despite whatever poetic turns of phrase might have crept in by way of the commandant, it was the most authentic available. As far as Spät's tale goes, in Stüssikofen he had boasted of a murder he had never committed, and in Munich Kohler had blamed the murder on someone he had wanted to get rid of along with the murdered man. I had the manuscript xeroxed. I found Dr.h.c. Isaak Kohler's address in the telephone book. I sent him the copy. Several days later I received a letter from Hélène Kohler. She asked me to pay her a visit. Her father's condition precluded her leaving home. I telephoned her. The next day I entered the Kohler estate.

It was as if I were walking into the manuscript, as if it were commenting on me as I approached the wrought-iron portal to the garden of the villa. Nature herself was redolent of wealth. The October flora was anything but shabby. The trees downright majestic. Still almost in summer glory. No foehn wind. Ingeniously trimmed hedges and bushes. Moss-covered statues. Naked, bearded gods with youthful rear ends and calves. Quiet ponds. A pompous pair of peafowl. Everything deathly still and eerie. Only a few birds could be heard. The house entwined with wild grape, ivy and roses, heavily gabled, large and roomy. Antique furniture, priceless pieces. Famous impressionists on the walls. Later I saw Old Dutch masters (an ancient maid led the way). I was left to wait in Dr.h.c. Isaak Kohler's den. The room was spacious. Gilded by the sun. Through the open French doors you could walk directly into the park. The two windows flanking the door went almost to the floor. Costly parquet. A giant desk. Deep leather armchairs. No pictures on the walls, just books to the ceiling. Every one of them a volume on mathematics or natural science, a considerable library. In a broad alcove, the billiard table, on which lay four balls. Through the open door, ancient Dr.h.c. Isaak Kohler came rolling, more delicate, more fragile, more transparent than ever, almost a phantom. He did not appear to notice me. He rolled over to the billiard table. To my amazement he climbed out of his wheelchair and began to play billiards. From a door at the rear came Hélène. Sporty—blue jeans, silk shirt, handknit sweater with three large red, blue, and yellow squares. She laid a finger to her lips. I understood. I followed her. A large drawing room. Another pair of open French doors. We sat down out on the terrace. Under an awning. The last time I've been able to sit outside this year. Old wicker chairs, an iron table with a slate top. A mower out on the lawn. The first piles of leaves. The peacocks among them. She said she had just been doing some gardening. A young fellow was turning over soil at the back of the park. Whistled as he worked. She was going to have to get rid of the peacocks. The neighbors were complaining. They had been complaining for fifty years now. But her father loved peacocks. She thought perhaps only because they annoyed the neighbors. He had simply let the peacocks scream. Despite the police, who had dropped by from time to time. Peacock screeches were the most ghastly thing you could ever hear. The houses all around them had declined in value because of the peacocks. The price of land had gone down. Her father had bought it all up. The neighbors no longer dared complain. Then she poured me some tea. Her father was a monster, I said. That might be, she said. Had she read the manuscript? Skimmed it, she answered. Spät had loved her, I remarked, he had had trouble writing about it, and she had loved him once too. Good old Spät, she said, the only person he ever loved was Daphne, his writing was liveliest when it was about her. He only imagined his love for her, Hélène. Had only imagined, I corrected her, good old Spät had died fourteen days before, in the Stüssi valley. "The tea's cold," she said, and tossed what was left in her cup across the terrace and onto lawn covered with yellow leaves, right at the feet of the young gardener, who happened to be passing by, whistling saucily.

Then the peacocks screeched. They normally didn't do that at this time of day, she explained, they would stop soon enough. But the peacocks didn't stop screeching. We had best go inside, she said, and we went inside, closed the French doors, sat down in two upholstered chairs, a small game table between us. Cognac? Gladly. She poured. The peacocks went on screeching outside, stubborn, eerie. Fortunately her father couldn't hear the beasts, she said, and she asked if I had read the part about the genuine Monika Steiermann. All of that seemed most improbable to me, I replied. She had been invited to see her once too, on a summer evening, Hélène said, she hadn't even been quite eighteen at the time and, like everyone else in the city, had thought Daphne was Monika Steiermann and had admired her, but had been jealous too, and had been jealous of Benno as well, because he had avoided her, and who all hadn't he seduced in those days, it had been downright chic to sleep with Benno, just as it had been chic to sleep with Monika Steiermann, although everyone was convinced that the two of them would marry, and that had been considered chic too, but she, Hélène, as Kohler's daughter, had been out of bounds. Benno had stayed clear of her. And yet she hadn't thought twice about accepting Steiermann's invitation, perhaps she had secretly hoped she would meet Benno there, that's how much of a crush she had had on him. She had told her father about it after dinner, over strong coffee. Her father had asked if she had been invited to the apartment on Aurorastrasse, and picked up the bottle of Marc, he always drank Marc at home. To Mon Repos, she had answered, no one had ever been invited there before. No, her father had replied, until now only he and Lüdewitz had been invited there. Might he give her some advice? She wouldn't follow his advice, she had rejoined stubbornly. She shouldn't accept the invitation, her father had said and finished off his Marc, that was his advice. But she had gone anyway. She had pedaled her bike to Wagnerstutz and had rung the bell at the entrance, after first leaning her bike against the iron fence, she went on to explain. She had been surprised when nothing happened. Then she had noticed that the large iron gate was unlocked, had opened it and walked into the park, but she had barely set foot in the park when she was overcome with inexplicable fear, she had wanted to go back, but the gate wouldn't open again. Whereas until now she had been hesitant in telling all this, from here on she spoke as if everything that went on had nothing to do with her but had happened to someone else. According to her report, she was aware from that moment on that she had been lured into a trap. The neglected park lay in the glow of an intense sunset, a stroke of burning red that seemed malicious somehow. Mechanically she made her way up toward the invisible villa. The gravel crunched beneath her feet. Then she noticed a garden gnome beside the path, then three, and then several of them peering through the stalks of the unmowed lawn, among lupines and larkspur, rank overgrowth of cosmoses, malevolent in the twilight, despite their chubby-cheeked faces, especially when she noted gnomes smoking pipes and grinning down at her from the trees; disgusted, she hurried past these gnomes, until she found herself opposite garden gnomes with large, almost bald, beardless heads—glazed ceramic figures larger than the other ones, about the size of four-year-old children. She had not dared to go past them, but then she noticed that one of these gnomes was winking at her; she stared in terror at the figure. The figure began to grin. She hurried up through the park, among squadrons of obscene garden gnomes, until she reached a meadow without any gnomes, a gentle slope from which the villa was visible above her. She stood there out of breath. She looked back, hoping she had been mistaken. It all seemed like a terrifying dream. Then she spotted the grinning gnome again, moving toward her with small tottering steps; she ran toward the villa, ran through the open front door, she heard the patter of running steps behind her, she ran through a vestibule, then through a hall with a crackling fireplace although it was summer, all empty, with just the patter of running steps behind her. She then found herself in a den, slammed the door behind her, bolted it, looked about her. She was alone. The walls were covered with photographs of Benno. She threw herself into a leather armchair. A strange, sweetish odor. She lost consciousness. Then she came to again, she said, continuing her tale. Four naked colossuses had her in their embrace. Their heads had been shaved bald, and they stank of olive oil. They were slippery as fish. She couldn't remember it all now. She fought back. Someone laughed. Then her thighs were wrenched apart. Professor Winter emerged, naked and pot-bellied. Above this lecherous faun she saw the garden gnome that had been pattering behind her. It was crouching atop a cupboard, and only then had she realized that it wasn't a garden gnome but some female creature lurking and gazing down from the cupboard, and that everything that was happening was happening only for the sake of this creature with the almost bald head of an adult and the body of a four-year-old, that she had chased her into the villa so that things that could not be perpetrated on the creature, but that she wished to have perpetrated on her, would be perpetrated on Hélène; and once Winter had taken her, first Benno and then Daphne threw themselves on her; she was overcome by her only weapon, lust, and the more immeasurable her lust grew, the more tortured were the eyes of the creature. Its whole body quivered, a boundless envy in its eyes, as if shaken by the misfortune of being excluded from the lust Hélène was experiencing while being raped by creatures at her command; until the creature screamed "Stop!" in utmost horror and broke into sobs. Hélène was set free, the creature was carried out, and she was alone again in the den. She gathered her clothes together, there were still embers in the hall fireplace, then groping her way through the vestibule and the pitch-black park, she arrived at the entrance gate. It had been unlocked, she said, concluding her report, and she had ridden her bike back home.

She fell silent. Did this not shock me? she then asked. "No," I said, "but a little more cognac would hit the spot." She poured some for me and for herself. When she had returned home, she said, her father had still been in his office. At his desk. He had barely looked up at her. She had told him everything.

Then he had walked over to the billiard table and begun to play. What else did she want? he had asked. Revenge, she had answered. "Forget the whole thing," her father had said. But she had insisted on revenge. He had stopped playing to look at her. He had advised her not to go, and she had gone. Her affair. No advice had to be followed, otherwise it would be an order. What had happened was unimportant, because it had happened. You had to shake off the things that happened to you, anyone who was unable to forget was simply throwing himself in the path of time and would be crushed. But she wanted her revenge, she had answered. "My child," her father had said, and it was the only time that he had ever called her that, what he had urged her to do had been advice, no more. She wanted revenge, fine, revenge she would have. His affair. Then he had placed four balls on the billiard table and took a shot, just one, first one ball hit the cushion, bouncing off it and hitting another ball in the pocket, Winter, her father had said; as the next ball had disappeared into a pocket, Benno, then Daphne, and when he had said Steiermann, the table had been empty. And herself? she had asked. She had been the cue, he had answered. He would need her only once. What was going to happen to them, she had asked. "They will die," he had answered. In the same sequence he had announced. She should go on to bed, he still had work to do.

This conversation, she added after a while as we sat over our third cognac listening to the balls bounce off one another in the next room, this conversation had haunted her memory far more than what had occurred at Mon Repos; she had turned off the light in her room and for a long while had watched the unmerciful stars in the endless night—stars indifferent to whether or not there was life upon this unutterably paltry nothing we call our earth, let alone to human fate, and then the suspicion had arisen within her that her father had wanted her to go, and had expected her curiosity to seduce her. But why had the dwarf chosen her? Was the humiliation intended for her, or for her father? If it had been intended for her father, why had he first advised Hélène not to take revenge? Had he merely been considering whether or not he wanted to take up the battle? But what was the point of this battle? Who was opposing whom? That there was something else, some considerably more important enterprise, behind this brick trust that her father was always joking about, and that from time to time he would mention that the future belonged to silicon, although everyone whom she asked and who had anything to say could only reply that they hadn't the vaguest what her father meant by that—all of this unsettled her. Was there perhaps a power struggle going on between him and Lüdewitz? Was what had happened to her simply Steiermann's signal to her father that she would no longer tolerate his interference?

I pondered all that she had told me. I was unclear about one thing, I said. Her father had told the story of the murder in Munich, fine, he had had to suggest the wrong motive, but that the idea of using the politician's revolver had first occurred to him only as he drove up in front of the Du Théâtre—no, that was totally improbable. Hélène looked at me attentively. Damn but she was a beautiful woman. That was correct, she said, her father had not been telling the truth. They had talked the murder over together. Poor Spät had guessed it. Her father had shot Winter with his own revolver and shoved the weapon into the minister's coat, which she had then removed from the pocket during the flight and had then tossed into the Thames in London. But the minister hadn't flown to London on Swissair, I interjected. Stüssi-Leupin's objection had been correct, she replied, but he could not have known that she had flown with the minister as his companion of choice. For just that reason, she had been his constant visitor at the private clinic. She fell silent. I gazed at her. She had her life behind her, and I mine behind me. "Spät?" I asked. She did not evade my eyes. I told her about my meeting with him. She listened. Spät had created for himself an image of her that was quite false, she said calmly, and I would create an equally false image of her. Within a few weeks after that night, she had begun an affair with Winter, then with Benno, which was the reason for Benno's argument with Winter and for Daphne's with Benno and for Daphne's breaking off with Steiermann—and as for who else had she slept with, that was a question of no importance, with everyone was relatively close to an exact answer. She was forever trying to explain rationally what was in fact irrational, but her behavior was stronger than her reason. Perhaps all of her explanations were only an attempt to justify her own nature, which had erupted that night at Mon Repos, perhaps she was simply longing to be raped again and again, she said, because a person was only truly free when being raped: free from her own will as well. But that, too, was just another explanation. The uncanny feeling that she had been nothing but a tool of her father's had never left her. All of the people he had named in his game of billiards had lost their lives in the predicted sequence, Steiermann last of all. Two years ago. On his advice, she had got involved in the armament business, which had been the ruin of Trög, Ltd. Then she had been found dead on her Greek island. Her four bodyguards had been riddled with bullets. Steiermann herself had not been found until six months later, head down in an olive tree. Hadn't I read about it? The name had meant nothing to me, I replied. When the news of Steiermann's disappearance had appeared in the newspapers, Hélène said, she had found a telegram on her father's desk, consisting of just a series of numbers, 1171953, which, if one read them as a date, referred to the night of her rape. If the murder had occurred on order of her father, however, who had carried that order out, and who had been behind the people who carried it out, and who behind them? And had Steiermann's death marked the end of a corporate war? And had that power struggle been something rational or irrational? What went on in that world? She didn't know. I didn't know either, I said.

"Let's return to Spät," I said, if she didn't mind. She didn't mind, she said, she had hoped that in taking on the commission her father had given him, Spät would clear it up. Clear what up? Clear up who had instigated her father to commit murder—herself. Not very logical, I said. Why is that? she answered, she might have put her father up to it. She could have made a choice. She was spinning in a circle, I declared, first she had assigned all the guilt to her father, now to herself. They were both guilty, she replied. That was splendidly crazy, I said. She was crazy, she replied. Go on, I demanded. She was not about to be unnerved. When, after her father's acquittal and subsequent departure, Spät had pounced on her, almost chancing on the truth, she had gone to the commandant and admitted everything. What did she mean by that, I asked. Admitted it, admitted everything, she repeated. And so? I asked. She fell silent. Then she said the commandant had asked her that too, And so? Then he had lit one of his cigars and said, Spilled milk. As had been subsequently determined, Benno had taken his own life, and as to who had fired the shot, or to go searching the Thames for the revolver, impossible, there were cases where the justice system made no sense, became mere farce. She should leave now, he would forget what she had told him. Why hadn't her father mentioned Spät even once? I asked. He had forgotten about him. Stüssi-Leupin too, I said. It was strange, she replied, how her father had taken it into his head that Benno and not he had committed the murder. She was the only person who still knew that her father had been the murderer. Did she know that for sure? I asked; it was rather probable, to be sure, but perhaps it had been Benno after all. She shook her head. It had been her father. She had examined the revolver that she took from the minister's coat pocket and had loaded it at home herself.

Why was she telling me all this? I asked. She looked at me in amazement. Why for heaven's sake had I sent her the manuscript? If not to get to the truth behind it all? I was a writer before anything else, who wasn't interested in other people's truth, only in my own; I was concerned about writing a novel, nothing else, and once the book was published, it would appear under my name, not under Spät's. Was the manuscript Spät's or mine? Only I knew that. I claimed I had got it from the commandant. She had known that old windbag too, he had often been a guest of her and her father, and had told tales out of school. He could have done that with me too. But if I was going to use her, then would I please not describe her like one of those sweet things in Goethe, all of whom should have their hides tanned, they were so boring, except for Philine, the only one of his creatures the old gentleman would have liked to sleep with. Then she stared ahead glassy-eyed. The young gardener walked past the window whistling. Could I find my own way out? I took my leave. The old man was still playing billiards in his study. *A la bande.*

Four minutes till two. I walk to the door of my study. When I had it designed, I could see the lake from here. Now trees block the view. I have had to cut down some that weren't even there when I first moved here. It's sad to have to cut down trees, to murder them. The oak has grown to a mighty tree. Those trees give me a sense of time, my time. Different from the sense of it I get by gazing at the sky. With some regret, I can now see the Pleiades, Aldebaran, Capella, winter stars, and yet it's still summer, an omen that I've grown older by a year in the space of four months. In the sky, objective time is unreeled, the measurable time of a man soon to turn sixty-five; with the trees time moves subjectively with me toward death, no longer measurable, only noticeable. But how does the earth sense time? I look out onto the lake by night; it has not changed, if one disregards what men have done to it. And yet how old does the earth sense itself to be? Objectively? Ancient? Four and a half billion years old? Or does it feel itself subjectively in the prime of life, since it may live on for another seven billion until the sun becomes a cinder. Or does it sense time racing by with lightning speed, does the earth feel itself as an impatient, violent force, boiling up, bursting continents apart, heaving mountains high, shoving layer atop layer, flooding the land with the sea; do we pass our lives on solid ground, or are we walking on shifting ground that at any moment may open up and swallow us? And what about humanity's time? We've divided it as objectively as possible into antiquity, the Middle Ages, modern times, postmodern times, and are awaiting ever newer times; and, of course, there are even more delicate divisions—for instance, the Age of the Greeks follows upon the Legacy of the East, is succeeded by Caesar and Christ, is followed by the Age of Belief; the Renaissance merrily rings in the Age of Reformation, and then the age in which Reason will rise up can no longer be held back, is still rising even now, it rises and rises. And let's not be small-minded: The first and second world wars and Auschwitz were episodes, Chaplin is better known than Hitler, only the Albanians still believe in Stalin, and a few Peruvian terrorists in Mao. Forty years of peace, that's what counts, not universal peace, granted, actually only between the superpowers and in Europe, in the Pacific too, for the most part, and in Japan, washed innocent of all guilt by Hiroshima and Nagasaki, and even China is opening up travel bureaus. And yet how does this peace, if it in any sense has the time to call itself such, experience its own time? Does time stand still for it, and if so, does it know what to do with it? Does time get away from it? Or does it perhaps sweep across peace like a storm wind, a tornado, slamming cars into one another, brushing trains from their tracks, flinging jumbo jets against mountains, burning cities to the ground? How does our time of forty measurable years of peace unroll objectively, our time, in which a real war, for which nations are arming, appears ever more inconceivable and yet is conceived? Has not our time of peace—for whose survival millions demonstrate, carry banners, sing pop songs, and pray—long since assumed the form of what we once called war, because to mollify ourselves we build catastrophes into our peace? World history dangles endless time before mankind. But perhaps for earth, measured objectively, it is only a short episode, not even that, an incident within an earth second, hardly detectable on a cosmic scale, barely leaving behind a meaningful dent. The Dorians believed that they had hardly sprung from the earth, were still stuck in the clay, when they fell upon one another. And thus, in reality, we fall upon one another, whether in peace or war, having barely escaped the Ice Age, men upon women, women upon men, men upon men, women upon women, guided not by reason but by instinct, the latter millions of years longer in development than the former, its motives inscrutable. And so, using the threat of atomic, hydrogen, and neutron bombs, we keep the worst at arm's length, like gorillas drumming on their chests to frighten other gorilla bands, all the while in danger of perishing of the peace we want to preserve, covered in death by the branches of dead forests. Wearily I return to my desk. Return to my battlefield, under the spell of my creatures, but not to another reality—except that since its time has run out, it is no longer ours. My own invention, and yet I have been unable to puzzle it out. My creatures created their own reality, which they snatched from my imaginative powers and thus from my reality, from the time I surrendered to create them.

And so they have become a part of our common reality and thus one of the possibilities, one of which we call world history—it too wrapped in the chrysalis of our fictions. And yet is this story, which became real only in my imagination and now, once written, slips away from me, any more pointless than world history, any less earthquake-proof than the ground on which we build our cities? And God? If we posit him, has he acted any differently from Dr.h.c. Isaak Kohler? Was not Spät free to turn down the job of seeking a murderer who did not exist? Did he not then have to find a murderer who did not exist, just as man, once he had eaten of the fruit of the tree of good and evil, had to find the God, who did not exist, or the devil? Is that not the fiction of God by which he justifies his wayward creation? Who is the guilty party? The one who commissions the job, or the one who takes it on? The one who forbids, or the one who disregards the prohibition? The one who passes the laws, or the one who breaks them? The one who allows for freedom, or the one who takes advantage of it? We are perishing of the freedom we permit others and ourselves. I leave my study, which is empty now, freed of my creatures. Four-thirty. In the sky I can see Orion for the first time. Whom is he chasing?

Friedrich Dürrenmatt
September 22, 1985

POSTSCRIPT

The Execution of Justice was begun in 1957. I planned to complete the novel in a few months. But then came the interruption of work on *Frank the Fifth*, and *The Execution of Justice* was put aside. Later attempts to take it up again failed, the last in 1980, when the intention was to make it the thirtieth volume in my collected works. But I could get nowhere with the development of the plot, had no notion of how I had once planned it. In the spring of 1985, Daniel Keel suggested that *The Execution of Justice* be published as a fragment. I reluctantly consented and then decided I would write one central chapter, but then began to rewrite the whole novel and to complete it, probably in a different way from what I had originally planned. Finally, my thanks to Charlotte Kerr, my wife. I am grateful to her for important dramaturgic pointers and for her constant critical attention to my writing.

Did you know?

Swiss writer Friedrich Dürrenmatt was one of the most highly regarded German-language novelists and dramatists of the twentieth century, and his works have been translated into 49 languages. As a dramatist he wrote plays that reflected the mood of a war-scarred Europe. As a novelist, he is famed for his philosophical crime thrillers, which draw comparisons to the works of Paul Auster and Umberto Eco for their post-modern questioning of the conventions of the genre.

Dürrenmatt thought detective novels should reflect the absurdity of real life rather than proceeding like mathematical equations with a definite solution. Of the traditional crime writers, he once said, "You set up your stories logically, like a chess game: all the detective needs to know is the rules, he replays the moves of the game, and checkmate, the criminal is caught and justice has triumphed. This fantasy drives me crazy."

Dürrenmatt's most famous novel, *The Pledge*, was initially written as a screenplay titled *Es geschah am hellichten Tag* (*It Happened in Broad Daylight*). The film producers compelled Dürrenmatt to bring this original to a neat conclusion that they felt was more suitable for the screen. The decidedly un-neat conclusion of the subsequent novel, and the subtitle *Requiem for the Detective Novel*, reflect Dürrenmatt's deep dislike of such formulaic and predictable plot constructions. Ironically, this book went on to spawn two successful movies, including a 2001 film starring Jack Nicholson and directed by Sean Penn.

ALSO AVAILABLE FROM PUSHKIN VERTIGO

FRIEDRICH DÜRRENMATT

PUSHKIN VERTIGO

SOME CRIMES LEAD TO JUSTICE. OTHERS TO MADNESS.

THE PLEDGE

'SPELLBINDING' WASHINGTON POST

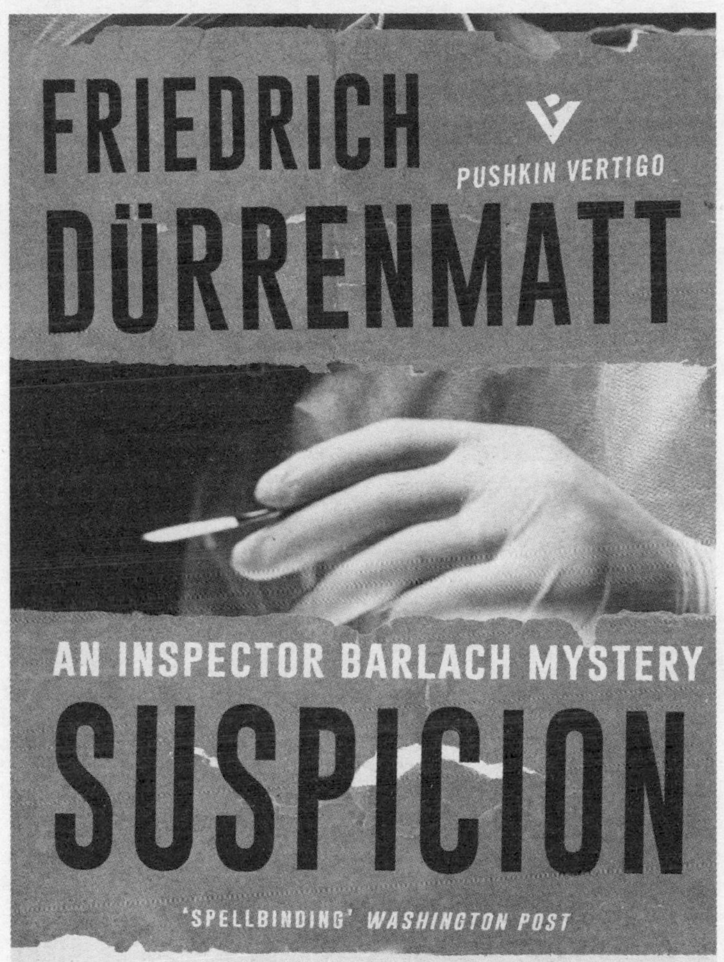
FRIEDRICH DÜRRENMATT
PUSHKIN VERTIGO
AN INSPECTOR BARLACH MYSTERY
SUSPICION
'SPELLBINDING' WASHINGTON POST